DEPTHS OF DECEPTION

Gripping psychological suspense

DIANE M DICKSON

Paperback published by The Book Folks

London, 2019

ISBN 978-1-80462-304-6

www.thebookfolks.com

For Ian

Chapter 1

It was one of those days that was wet before it started. Before the grey light had leached into the morning it was already sodden. Jed arrived at the measly two sides of Perspex that made up the bus shelter, soaked. His short black jacket was showerproof but this wasn't a shower. The damp had already worked its way through the fabric of his M & S suit and made it as far as his shirt, turning the crisp cotton into a crinkled rag. His trousers were wet almost to his knees and the rain had seeped into his shoes, chilling his feet and turning his socks into unfriendly wet wraps.

He swiped at the water that dripped from his fringe onto his lashes and leant forward to peer into the rain-washed distance. The number three, often unreliable, would no doubt be totally absent today. He heaved a sigh, blowing air through his nostrils and dragged a mobile from his pocket. There was a message from Bella, two words: *No thanks*. Okay that relationship was a squib as damp as the morning and he might just as well let it go. In fairness, he'd seen it coming and now most of what he felt was relief.

He perched on the tiny plastic seat and waited with elbows on his knees, chin on his fists and his spirit somewhere down in his damp footwear.

The seat jerked and he cast his eyes to the side. Black opaque tights and ankle boots rapidly being ruined by the rain. A short denim skirt patched with damp, he slid his eyes on upwards. A black leather jacket, water running in tiny cascades across the front. Further up still, dark rat's tails of hair dripping onto narrow shoulders.

She was grinning as he raised his gaze to her face, and she lifted her arms and shook them. Water shot from the sleeve ends and she laughed aloud as he leaned away raising a hand in defence.

"Hey, you're wet already, a bit more won't make any difference."

He smiled back at her. "I guess not. Bloody horrible morning!"

"No, not really," she said. He blinked and pulled back his head. "It's wet alright, but that's not horrible, it's just wet."

"Yeah right." He looked away now, irritated by her response.

"You going to work?" she asked him.

"Yes. You?"

"Uh-hu, not me."

"You didn't need to, but you still came out in this?"

"Yeah. Out's good. Where do you work then?"

"Bailey and Herriot. Estate agents." He waited for the sarcastic sneer and knowing look, but her response surprised him.

"Oh cool, houses and flats?"

"Yes, and some offices."

"That must be fun, looking around other people's places."

She had thrown him. He had no illusions; he knew the general public regarded estate agents as little better than investment bankers, but her eyes were alight with interest.

"Well, it can be."

It wasn't, it was mostly frustrating and often disappointing, but her eyes asked for fun and he felt compelled to provide it. "Some of the more valuable properties, you know, the bigger houses, that's fun, but we do handle some really grotty places as well."

"Still, peeking into private lives – it's got to be interesting."

"I guess so – sometimes anyway."

"You worked there long?"

"Nearly five years."

"Oh, you must be pretty senior then."

He didn't answer for a moment. Was this friendly teasing or was she being sarcastic? She was sitting with him at a rain-soaked bus stop at half past eight on a late autumn morning; he was dressed in a cheap suit and a short jacket. Did she really believe he was a senior member of staff at one of the most prestigious real estate agencies in the town? He didn't think so.

"Yeah right." He turned away.

"Sorry, did I say something wrong?"

When he turned back, her expression was openly puzzled. Maybe she wasn't being derogatory, maybe she really didn't understand about four-wheel drive cars and bespoke tailoring and the way you had to earn them.

"No, not really. I'm a junior agent. Five years is not that long you know and I'm still training."

"Oh sorry. I didn't mean anything, I just thought, you know – five years seems a long time."

"Not really, and as I say I'm still training. Part-time course. Surveying. At the college."

"Cool."

"Anyway, here's my bus. Nice to meet you, have a good day."

She grinned at him again and raised a hand, an almost wave. He climbed into the steamy fug and flashed his travel pass. By the time he'd reached the seat at the back, she had left the bus stop and was walking slowly down the road. She walked with her head up letting the rain soak her hair and face, and as the bus passed, she turned and grinned at him again. He sat for a while with the answering grin on his face.

* * *

I'm cold, I'm frightened. I think it's morning but it's always dark so I can't be sure. There is no sound. Am I alone again? I don't want to be alone again. I ache and the room is spinning whenever I move my head.

Chapter 2

There was no reason to suppose the girl would be there again. She hadn't ever been there on the countless other mornings. Even the previous day, it seemed that she had merely taken refuge from the rain. She hadn't waited to catch a bus. Nevertheless, Jed watched out for her, not in an open watchful way, but simply scanning the few people out and about.

She didn't come and he climbed onto the number three fighting a feeling of disappointment.

It was a good morning at work. They took on several new properties, and even better, they completed on two. Final and completed, and money in the bank. The downside was that neither of them were his, but on the other hand, they were important properties so there would be drinks at lunchtime in the pub.

"So, how's tricks, Jed?" He'd tried to avoid Steven, but now found himself standing at the bar with the senior agent who was the supervisor of his section.

"Yeah fine thanks. You?"

"Oh yes, things are looking good. Two viewings this afternoon over at The Park," he said, naming the prestigious new development they had been commissioned to handle.

"Great. Big ones, are they?"

"Yeah, both on the side near the woods, six beds, five baths. They're selling very fast. Of course, you haven't actually got any of those have you?"

"No." Sod him, he knew full well what was in Jed's portfolio. "Bit of a coup for Simon – Brestwick Hall. Lucky him finding that hotel developer."

"Ah, luck has nothing to do with it mate. It's all about who you know. Networking, that's the key."

"Right, anyway better get these drinks over to the table eh, Samantha looks as though she's spitting feathers."

"Off you go then, Jed. Oh, before you go, any movement on that little place down the High Street?"

"No, afraid not, it's pretty naff you know. There's damp and the wood's rotten in most of the windows."

"Ah well, do what you can eh. Got to go over now and hobnob with Simon and Charles." With that he swaggered off with a bottle of Moet and four glasses towards the table where the partners were sitting with the new owner of Brestwick Hall, a huge country pile that was now earmarked for development into a 'boutique' hotel and spa. Jed picked up the tray and joined the others in the window.

Samantha reached across the table to take her glass from his hand and frowned at him. "You okay, Jed? You look like a wet weekend."

"Yeah I'm fine, just bloody Simon blowing his own trumpet again."

"Oh, don't take any notice."

"I know, but he's such a prick. He knows that place down the High Street is going to take forever to sell and yet he's always rubbing it in. He's got two more properties over at The Park as well, more high commission work."

"Hey, come on, give it time. You do okay."

"I suppose, but sometimes I get sick of handling the crud. You know Cheshire is a wealthy part of the UK, there are dozens of really brilliant properties all over the county, so why do I only get the run-down, fag end places?"

"Yeah, but Jed, we all know how it feels. Until I went into the commercial section, I got all the nasty little places. Just bide your time. Anyway, you've got exams coming up soon, haven't you?"

"Yeah."

"How's that going then?"

"Okay, I've enjoyed the course, I reckon I'll be okay. I'll be glad when it's all done though." The pretty blonde raised her glass and glanced around the table.

"Good luck then, I hope you ace it and then you can set up your own business and we'll all come and work for you and you can turn down Simon." Jed grinned as the little group clinked their glasses. He glanced over to the partners' table. One day, one day he'd be sitting there.

Chapter 3

"Hiya."

Jed spun around to see the girl hanging onto the corner post of the bus stop. She was leaning in and swinging back and forth a little.

"Oh hello."

"Dry today then. That make you happier?"

"Hmm at least I won't have to sit in the office in wet socks." He grinned.

"Did you have a good week?"

"Yeah, blimey is it a week since?"

"Since what?" He could have bitten off his tongue. He didn't want her to know he'd thought about her, watched for her every morning.

"Since I saw you?" It was the only way to answer.

"Yeah – a week."

"Is it your day off again?"

"No – I'm just going to the newsagents. I saw you, thought I'd come over and say hello."

"Ah right. Do you work locally then?"

She'd slipped into the shelter and dragged a small box from her pocket. She took out a spliff and lit up. He had to admit he was impressed at her nerve, her total confidence. She offered him some but he held up his hand, shook his head. She drew on the skinny joint, screwing up her eyes from the smoke. "Well do you? Work round here?" He was nervous on her behalf, there was no-one in the shelter just then but plenty of people passing.

"Yeah, oh look here's your bus. The number three, right?"

"Yes, yes that's it."

"See ya." And she was gone. By the time the bus pulled away from the stop she was already out of sight inside the little shop.

She was cute, there was something about her that appealed to him in spite of the marijuana. She gave the impression of being amused by everything. Probably what his mother would have called flighty really. Not like Laura his oh so perfect sister, apple of his parents' eyes. Laura with her degree in biology and her job at the hospital. Laura with her oh so serious boyfriend Gavin, who worked in the same place.

He sighed. It wasn't Laura's fault, but she made him feel as though he was failing. He knew he should stop comparing himself to her, to people at work, to so-called celebrities but it all seemed to be taking so much time. In spite of what he'd said, it did seem like years and years since he'd left school and started working at the office and he was still in college and still earning a skinny wage and living at home.

He wondered briefly where she lived. She couldn't live around here surely. The houses in this area were all upwards of half a million, most of them much more and she had looked... a bit shabby. Mind you he lived here, him with his measly salary and his well-to-do mum and dad, so maybe she also lived at home with parents. It appealed; he'd have nothing to live up to with her. They'd be the same. Yes, it appealed.

What was he doing? He didn't even know her name. He'd seen her a couple of times at the bus stop. Still she had something. She made him smile. Smiling on the bus to work, right, that'd have to stop; people would think he was a weirdo.

* * *

I need to drink but can't reach the water. I feel useless tears trickle down my cheeks and into my ears. I disgust myself with the smell of my space. Crying won't help but what more can I do except to pray for the end?

Chapter 4

Another frustrating two hours spent showing people round a property they never had any intention of buying. More and more, Jed was becoming convinced that he had made a dreadful error with his choice of career.

He could have done something else, his A-levels had been good enough. It had just seemed so easy. He'd seen the programmes on the television and watched the glamorous presenters searching out houses for rich clients. He had seen them travelling to Europe and beyond, all expenses paid to find 'A Place in France' or 'A Villa in Italy', and here he was brewing a cup of instant coffee after trudging round a run-down semi with a cheap kitchen and plastic window frames.

He sighed.

"Do you have any idea how often you do that?" He turned to find Samantha leaning against the door frame, grinning at him.

"Do what?"

"That sigh. Blowing through your nose like that. Like a pissed off dragon."

"Heh, right – do I?"

"Yeah. Make us a cup will you? I have to go out in a quarter of an hour and I don't think I'll get another chance."

"Right."

"Is everything alright?" she asked. "You know, with the big sigh and all."

"Oh yes, it's just one of those days, I guess. Nothing seems to be moving and I'm feeling a bit frustrated. Plus, I've got my first exam tomorrow. I'm not really worried but –" He shrugged his shoulders.

"Yeah, I know. You'll be fine though. I'm sure you will."

Jed handed her the mug of coffee and squeezed past her on his way back to his desk. He glanced up at the window just in time to see a girl outside turn and walk away. He peered across the office. Was it her? The black jacket looked familiar and the dishevelled fall of dark hair, but he couldn't be sure. For a moment he thought about running out into the street, going after her. It was ridiculous of course. He turned back to his desk and picked up the phone to make a report on the viewing. Time to sell some good spin to the hopeful owners of the run-down semi. He sighed and then grinned as Samantha raised her eyebrows at him as she walked by.

"Day off tomorrow, Jed?" Steven paused on the way out of the office.

"Yes, that's right. Exam."

"If you get a chance after that, we could do with updating the particulars of 15 Old Road and the offices at The Marlins."

"Oh, but I've booked the whole day. It's unpaid leave. I thought that was the usual deal."

"You won't get on if you don't put in the time now will you mate? Up to you of course, but it'd look better if you did some work as well. You could always do it at home and send them in for Molly to print off and upload to the website."

"Right, right I'll do that then." So that was it, the plan for a trip to see his sister was finished, and by suggesting he do it at home Steven had taken advantage of the unpaid time. He grabbed his jacket from the back of his chair and stormed out. It wasn't finishing time, but he knew anger would get in the way of him doing any more meaningful work.

He stalked to the stop and for once the bus was on time. He clambered aboard and flung himself into the first empty place.

"Finishing early?" The girl plonked down on the adjoining seat and grinned at him, brown eyes twinkling.

"Yeah."

"So, you please yourself then do you?"

"No – not really it's just – oh I was pissed off to be honest, with my boss so I decided to call it a day."

"Oh right. Is he a pig then – your boss?"

"He's a bit of a wanker sometimes and he just made me mad."

"Right – pub then?"

"What?"

"We should go to the pub – have a drink – slag him off. It'll make you feel better."

"Are you not working?" As he said it, he had the sudden thought that maybe she was out of work and he'd put her on the spot, but she just shook her head. "Oh right. Okay then, why not?"

* * *

Someone has been today, someone has been. The place has been cleaned a little. I must have been deeply asleep. How can that be, that they can do all this without me knowing? My head is hurting again and my vision is blurred. There is juice though, and a small sandwich. It's dry and dull but it's good to eat something.

Chapter 5

"How did it go, Jed?"

"Morning Samantha – yes I think it went well. I did some back checking when I got home, and I think I did okay."

"Great – when's the next one?"

"Two days. Then the final one next week on Wednesday and then the wait."

"Have you got plans for afterwards?"

"How do you mean?"

"When you get your quals? What are you going to do? Are you moving on or hoping for a few more years here?"

"I guess I want to stay here for a bit longer at least. Get more experience and then…"

"The ship's pretty full here just now isn't it? There's not much chance for promotion, not unless someone bumps off Steven, which is not impossible."

Samantha was grinning at him, but his stomach had tied in knots. She was right, he had been lazy and let things slide. What was the point in all the study and the exams if in the end he would just be coming in every day, sitting at the same desk and handling the same cruddy houses and flats?

He felt depressed and a bit stupid. Samantha had a very specific career plan that involved her getting a job in London and, although she had made no secret of it, the firm had kept her on. She was too good to let go until she made the decision. That was what he should be aiming at – making an impression and ensuring that he was noticed.

He fiddled with the pens on his desk and answered a couple of emails. There was an appointment in the early afternoon and then nothing booked. It wasn't very inspiring. He was marking time, wasn't he? He looked around the office. Four other agents in his section and all of them with more properties and more earning potential than him. Even Dave, the sixty year old was selling more, acquiring more instructions, and thus making more money.

It was time to get things sorted. He had to have a plan and start to make waves. He walked across to the property boards. The cheap little places were at the far end of the office away from the door. He went to the premier section, the houses with swimming pools and paddocks and sweeping driveways. That was where the money was. Though none of them were actually "his" that didn't mean he couldn't work on them, see if he could find some interest. He should go to the golf club with his dad. The very thought bored him rigid, but it was the sort of place to see and be seen. He should start going to some of the events at the Chamber of Commerce. It was time to mix with movers and shakers. He needed to get his arse into gear and begin to make some serious money.

"Lusting after a seven bedroom country home eh, Jed?"

"Oh, hi Steven, just looking, you know. Just keeping up to date."

"Good man."

Jed hissed under his breath as his supervisor clapped him on the shoulder and then swaggered off to his small, glass-walled office, stopping on the way to chat to the secretary.

Chapter 6

The exams were over. Jed had enjoyed the course, it was interesting and played to his strengths, and the day to day experience in the agency had added another dimension.

Work was still a trudge though, and now there was the constant niggle of what to do about his future. While he was at college, he could tell himself he was moving forward, but now it was over he had been swept by the realisation that he was stuck.

"Hey gloomy, wassup?"

"Hi Libby." After the session at the pub they met often in the mornings. She would plonk down on the seat beside him, light up a spliff and sit and chat until his bus came. He looked forward to it. "No, nothing really. Just thinking, you know, about the future. I've finished at the college and I need to start to move along. I need to start earning some serious money."

She raised her eyebrows, tipped her head to one side, the question implicit in her actions. "How are you gonna do that then?"

"Important properties, that's the way. I need to start handling some really good properties. Big houses, estates, that sort of thing!"

"Well, you work in an estate agents, what's the problem?"

"Ha, yeah. You have to prove yourself. You have to show 'em that you can move them along."

"So?"

"So, first of all you have to get them and you can't do that until you prove yourself. It's a vicious circle. You need clients who want you personally to do the work for them. Networking, that's the key. You have to meet the right people and make the right impression."

"Can't you do that then? You said your mum and dad are pretty rich."

"Did I?"

"Yeah in the pub. You said your dad was on the committee at the golf club and your mum was minted."

"I did not." He nudged her with his arm, that mischievous glint in her eye delighted him. "I said my mum didn't work."

"Same thing, innit?"

He couldn't deny it. His family were well off with money on both sides, and his dad had a successful career as an accountant and tax advisor.

"I suppose. It takes time though, to build up your contacts."

"They should help you, your mum and dad. Why don't they?"

"I don't know – no. I have to do it myself don't I? I mean they looked after me when I was a kid, paid for school, all that stuff. I'm on my own now. That's right isn't it? I still live there yeah, but only until I get sorted."

She shrugged. "Seems odd to me but then – I never had much family."

She had told him nothing about her life, past or present. He had asked about her work, but she would say only that she worked as 'a sort of caretaker'.

"Anyway, what about you? You busy?" he asked.

"Oh, same old stuff, you know. Just moving dirt and weeding paths."

"Do you fancy a drink later, after work?"

"No, not today – I can't. Tomorrow though, tomorrow – I'll meet you outside your office."

"Oh okay."

* * *

I am disoriented again, the room spins and tips. I can't keep awake. I have slept I know, and while I slept, they have cleaned. I don't know who comes, but it is when I am asleep and I sleep so much.

Chapter 7

"You're miles away, you'll miss your bus if you don't watch out." Jed hadn't seen her approach and jumped a little with shock as Libby landed on the seat beside him.

"Hello. Yeah, I've got an appraisal today with the partners. An assessment and what they called a 'chat' about my future development."

"Oh cool."

"No, not really. I'm a bit worried they're going to tell me I'm out."

"How do you mean out?"

"Out, you know, sacked."

"No shit, can they do that?"

"Yes of course they can. It's their business. They can do what they like, and to be honest with the way things are in the property market at the moment we are probably over-staffed."

"Yeah but why you? You just took your exams and everything didn't you?"

"Yes, but that doesn't matter. It's all about the bottom line, bringing in the money, and I'm not."

"I thought you sold that house last week?"

"I did, I am selling bits and pieces but it's all just small potatoes."

"Oh, so you sell veg as well?"

"Ha ha, aren't you the witty one this morning." He leaned and gave her a little push. Her jacket sleeve wrinkled up her forearm revealing red wheals and scratches."

"Shit, what did you do?"

"What?" She glanced down. "Oh that, it's nothing, just stuff from work, gardening and what have you."

"Blimey, you should get danger money."

"Yeah, bloody right. Anyway, what about you and your assessment? What would make a difference?"

"Oh, nothing that I can do much about right now. I need to move things up a notch or two. Get some good stuff. I've tried, I went to an event with my dad, hobnobbed with some of the toffs, but you just have to be in the right place at the right time."

"Like when someone has a place to sell?"

"Yeah that's it. Listen, it might all be okay. I don't know, maybe it is just what they said it is – a chat about my future."

"If it's not – if they do give you the push, what will you do then?"

Jed shrugged and shook his head. "I don't know. I suppose I'd have to move away. Go up to London if I could find work there or just rethink the whole damn thing. Shit."

"Oh, come on, don't be down. Hey, what if you could tell them you might have a big deal coming up soon? You know make 'em think that they have to keep you on because there is something brewing?"

"Yes, of course, but I haven't. That's the problem."

"Do you know The Willows?"

"That great big place over by the river, yeah."

"That's where I work."

"Oh right."

"Thing is, I heard they might be selling that."

"Who might?"

"Well duh, the owners."

"Bloody hell, really? Who owns it now?"

"Some posh family. Anyway, I could sort of put your name in with them couldn't I, the family?"

He didn't want to burst her bubble of enthusiasm but as she sat there in front of him, her nails chipped and bitten and her hair in need of a wash, the thought that she could put his name forward to anyone of consequence was laughable. He was kind though.

"That'd be brilliant. Really great, yeah, I'd appreciate that."

"Okay then," she said, and suddenly the morning was a little better.

* * *

My arms hurt and my face is sore. Something has hurt me. I can't remember, was there a conflict of some sort, a struggle? And my hair – I have been shaved. When I rub my hand across my skull there is stubble, short and stark. It is shocking, though in truth now that the knots and tangles have gone, I feel cleaner. The rancid smell of grease has been replaced by a cleaner one. I am the shorn lamb. How can this have happened? How can my world, so warm and blessed have become so dark and hateful? What did I do wrong? I have bruises on my hands; I can see them in the dim light, dark roses blooming against the snow. My head is throbbing. At least I have juice to drink. It's sweet but the aftertaste is bitter. I can't tell what the flavour is, maybe it is grapefruit, or some artificial concoction.

Chapter 8

"Come in, Jed, sit down. Have you had your coffee or would you like one?"

"No thanks I'm fine, Mr Bailey."

"Excellent. Well, this shouldn't take too long. Mr Herriot is out of the office today so it's just going to be us two."

"Oh – right." He was struggling to keep his hands still, they wanted to wring together. His palms were damp. He tried to appear relaxed but had perched too far forward on the chair and now didn't know how to slide backwards without looking as though he was fidgeting. His throat prickled, he tried to clear it quietly. Simon Bailey raised his eyes from the folder he was reading and glanced across the gleaming wood of his desk.

"Would you like some water?"

"Erm, no hmm. Oh actually, yes please."

"Help yourself." The older man waved a hand in the direction of the side table. There was juice and sparkling water in bottles and a thermos of coffee. Jed leaned to the jug of still water and poured a small amount into a tumbler. His hand shook as he poured. He sipped. Normally the partners were friendly and approachable but there was something in the air today, something that made his stomach churn and his neck itch under the stiff collar.

When he sat back down, he slid a little further back on the leather seat – damn it they were uncomfortable chairs. In the corner of the office was a group of small settees around a low coffee table, the area for informal chats with clients and where the staff gathered for drinks at closing time on Christmas Eve. This though, this was formal and intimidating and he wanted it over. He wanted to know if he'd still have a job at the end of the month and, if he did, just what it was going to be leading to, if anything.

His boss laid a hand on the file and looked up, he smiled. "How are your parents, Jed?"

"Fine, they're fine thank you."

"Good, excellent. I played a round with your father a couple of weeks ago, he beat me again." A quiet laugh followed, but it didn't hide the message – I am friendly with your father. He and I go back a long way and I gave you this job because he put your name forward.

"Right, yes – he said he'd seen you." Jed found himself nodding and felt like a stuffed puppy in the back window of a car, he had to stop. He nodded a couple more times, when he raised his eyes it was to find Mr Bailey watching him, his eyebrows raised quizzically.

"Now then. I see you have finished at the college, yes?"

"Yes, sir."

"Oh, now come on, Jed, no need for formality. You know we don't expect that sort of thing from our team."

"No, sir, sorry s.. erm yes. I've finished yes."

"How did it go?"

"I think it went okay thank you. I have a good projected result. I have been in the top five percentile all the way through."

"Excellent. And, in the office, how do you think things are going downstairs?"

"Oh okay, yes I think it's all going fine. Steven seems happy enough."

"Yes – I've spoken to Steven of course." He lowered his gaze and turned over a couple of pages. He nodded. He frowned.

"I don't think there are any problems. If there are, he hasn't said anything."

"Quite, quite, yes well there we are. Have you given any thought to what you are going to do next?"

"Next?"

"Yes, now that your exams are over what are your plans?"

"I erm. I thought maybe I would give it a few more years, get some more experience before I decide whether to erm, maybe specialise in some way."

"I see. Nothing more concrete?"

"Naturally I would like to handle more prestigious properties, perhaps look to specialise on the farms perhaps or some of the bigger houses. Up to now I have only been assigned the smaller, less valuable listings. Of course, I realise that everyone has to do that. I'm not complaining, it's just that I do feel that I'm ready to move up a gear."

"Oh, I see. I assume you realise that the property market is still very difficult."

"Oh yes, I read the trade magazines of course, though things are looking up, aren't they?"

"In some areas."

God this was awful. He was getting no real feedback, no indication of how it was going or even an idea of what he had been called in to hear.

Mr Bailey linked his fingers together on the desk in front of him. He raised his eyes to meet Jed's. *Oh, here it comes.*

"As you know, Jed, we are very fully staffed."

"Yes, sir."

"We have been reasonably satisfied with your performance, to an extent. We've had no complaints as such. I'm going to be honest with you though, Jed." He leaned away from the desk, smiled a little – sugar with the medicine. "You haven't sparkled. I was rather hoping for something more from you, more flair – do you understand?"

"Flair, right. Oh, I don't really know – I mean – it's been difficult only handling the small places and there are so many agents and only so much property available." As he said it, he knew he was digging a great big hole and jumping in with both feet and a shovel.

"Yes, exactly. In times such as these, we need everyone to put in that extra effort. Do you understand? Good isn't enough, we need excellent."

"Yes, sir of course and now my exams are out of the way I'm ready to throw myself right into it."

The boss simply tipped his head to one side. The silence grew – and grew.

"I'm sorry you've been disappointed with my work."

"Not disappointed, Jed. Not so much disappointed as hmm, what shall I say? Under-impressed, yes. We have had a chat, Simon, Steven and myself, and we think that maybe you've allowed yourself to coast a little, perhaps assume advantages that weren't really there. Family associations and so on."

"I don't think that's true, it's just the exams recently and erm..."

"Yes, but they're only a part of the whole picture, aren't they?"

Jed could only nod. His heart was on the floor; he was about to be left with no choice, wasn't he? He was going to have to leap before he was pushed, he wasn't ready to resign. He had nowhere to go.

Unless.

"Actually, I am really glad we have had this opportunity to talk, sir."

"Oh." The older man was thrown for a moment, hadn't expected to have the ball snatched from his hand. He waited.

"Yes, I've been intending to come and speak to you. I don't want to go over Steven's head with this, but I just thought that it might be something I should speak to someone more senior about."

"Oh?"

"Yes. The Willows."

"The estate by the river?"

"Yes, that's it."

"What about it?"

"I have heard, from a reliable source." What was he doing? A reliable source – really. "It may be available shortly."

"Really?" Simon leaned forward, a spark in his eye that hadn't been there moments before.

"Yes, and this person, erm this source has access to the family. Well, not to put too fine a point on it I think it may be possible that they will be happy for me to act for them – when the time comes that is."

"Aha, now that is interesting. Very interesting indeed. Right. For the time being let's keep this quiet. I'm sure you are aware of how the jungle drums can spoil a deal. Keep me informed and we'll see how we go. That is very interesting news indeed. A place like that. I don't need to tell you what sort of figures we're talking about – right? Do let me know about your results when they come in now won't you? Best to your parents. Thanks for coming in for this chat."

Jed sat at his desk, his head in his hands. The others left him alone believing they knew what had happened. They were already planning the whip-round for his leaving present. Right at that moment, a whip-round and a leaving present would have been the most welcome thing he could think of. He couldn't believe what he had just done, and what an idiot he had just made of himself.

Chapter 9

He shouldn't have gone to the stop so early. Libby always arrived around the same time – just a few minutes before his usual bus was due. Sometimes they barely had time to say hello and he left her sitting at the stop finishing her smoke. Then there were days when the bus was late and they had a chat and a bit of a laugh. So, all he had done by coming early today was to give himself longer to wait. He earned some odd looks from other people who clambered aboard the early bus while he stared at his phone and tried to look as though he had everything under control.

She had to come. But she didn't come every day, and he had no idea what the deciding factors were. Certainly not the weather, no matter if it was raining or sunny or blowing a hoolie she might turn up. She was always dressed in her ankle boots, thick black tights, a short skirt and the leather jacket. Now and again she would have a scarf wound round her neck, or her head or just wherever she had decided to put a bit of colour but that seemed random and unplanned.

His leg jigged up and down and he shuffled and shrugged his shoulders. *Please come, please, please come.* And there she was.

"Hiya." She swung round the end of the shelter and flopped onto the little yellow seat. "How are ya?"

"I'm fine – good thanks. You?"

"Oh yeah. So wassup?" she asked.

"How do you mean? Nothing, no it's fine. Why should there be anything wrong?"

"Hey, chill. I just meant – well you know – what are you doing – how are things going?"

"Oh yeah, right – course. Fine, things are fine."

"It doesn't look like it – you're well hyper."

"No, no I'm not."

"So, what's with the piston leg thing then?"

He glanced down, pressed a hand on his knee. She lit up her joint.

"Do you have to do that?" he asked.

"What?"

"That. Don't you worry?"

"Worry?"

"Yes, you know, worry that it might affect you. Make you – oh I don't know – unreliable?"

She spurted with laughter. "This?" She waved the skinny spliff in front of him. "This isn't going to make me anything. It has less effect than a couple of glasses of booze. Don't be a moron."

"It's just that every time I see you, here, you're smoking."

"Yeah well it's my morning treat isn't it. Anyway, I guess it's none of your business Mr Moody."

"No, no of course it's not – I'm sorry. I'm a bit uptight – you're right."

She peered at him. "You know this is nothing, it's barely a drug. If you want something that's really gonna have an impact you want something more than weed."

"Oh, I don't want anything."

"No, I know duh brain – all I'm saying is, this is nothing. I can tell you about stuff that would really give you a reason to worry. Stuff to get you high, stuff to bring you down and stuff to get you so fried you don't know whether you're here or hanging from a kite on Jupiter. Have you never done stuff?"

"Yes of course I have. I've smoked now and again, but I don't like it. I don't like to risk loss of control."

"Ha, sometimes it's not about the loss of control."

"What do you mean?"

"Oh nothing – look, things are getting heavy. Let's leave it. I smoke, it's not your problem."

"Yes, you're right. Sorry." She shrugged and inhaled deeply.

This wasn't the way he expected the morning to go and it wasn't helping him.

"Look, there's something I need to talk to you about."

"Oh right – looks like it'll have to wait. Here comes your bus." With a quick grin and a wave of her hand she pushed up from the seat and crossed the road. She didn't look back and he wasn't sure whether they were at odds or not. He needed her on his side. If there was even the slightest chance that she could help him she really had to be on his side.

* * *

Someone came just after I woke. I have no sense of time, but I think it is morning. It's dark with the drapes closed and now that my sight is weak, it is hard to tell whether or not I know them. It could be the same one each time, I think maybe it is. The agency used to send such pleasant girls. I wonder what has happened to them.

This one was, as always, quick and rough and silent. They no longer wear a uniform, everything is so casual, careless. There was no conversation. She cleared away the mess from the night. The stench is less when that has gone but always there is an air of decay and despair. So many things confuse me and it seems impossible. I don't know how long it has been like this or when it changed. I know that my life was other, and I remember things that happened so long ago, but they sadden me and I can't bear it. I don't remember how I came to this disability.

I feel so very alone. Where have they gone, the people who loved me?

I had a tray with toast and tea and later my sheets were changed. It is bliss. I am thankful for such small, small things. Soon after my head began to spin and I have been woozy ever since but at least I am lying on a clean sheet. I am so weak. I would try to move about just a little, but when I stand the room tilts and tips and nausea threatens. Best to sleep.

Chapter 10

"So, are you going to talk about it?" Samantha leant against the corner of Jed's desk. She fiddled with the pot holding paperclips. He could tell she was uncomfortable and the others were glancing at them from their various stations around the office.

"Talk about what?"

"You know what – your interview." He frowned at her and shook his head. "Fine, be that way. I was just trying to be supportive but, you know, please yourself."

"Sorry, sorry Sam. I'm just – oh, I can't talk about it just now."

"Fine. We're all in this together you know, Jed, and we were worried about you. We obviously shouldn't have bothered." She spun away, grabbed her jacket from the coat rack and slammed out of the office. The others all found deeply interesting articles to read on their computers or messed about with papers that needed sorting.

Oh well done, Jed, now you've got everyone in the office hating you, oh yes well done. In a flush of frustration and embarrassment he shrugged into his jacket and grabbed his mobile. He turned to the reception desk. "I've got some viewings, Molly. I'll be out for a couple of hours." He stormed into the street and walked towards the shopping mall. He did have a couple of appointments, but he was far too early. He could have done an inspection at some of the offices, but he had forgotten to sign out keys.

Could the day get any more difficult?

There was nothing he could do about The Willows just now, not until the morning. And even then, he would have to wait and see if Libby came to the bus stop. If she didn't, if he had really offended her with his comments, he was screwed. He was probably screwed anyway; the chances of anything coming of her throwaway comments were negligible.

There were two options. He could see the partners and tell them the deal had come to nothing. Okay, he would look a bit of an idiot but it happened often and they knew that. Then it was going to be an uphill struggle. He was already on the shortlist for the boot and once they knew he wasn't going to bring in a huge deal it would be the end. Of course, there was always a third way and that was for him to actually find a property. Something huge and expensive. He let his mind wander around the select areas. The Willows was the peach, there was no doubt. Hidden behind stone walls and with a grand entrance not much could be seen from the road, but he knew it was an imposing house with outbuildings and massive grounds.

He would go and have a look, just walk past. He had thought, the last time he had been down that way, it was all looking a bit shabby. He remembered that there were weeds growing around the gate posts. The lawns weren't as pristine as they had been. It didn't matter because the chances were, it wouldn't sell to a family. No, a developer would snap it up. Then there would be a wrangle about whether or not it could be turned into a small development of houses or, always the other option, a country hotel and spa, a conference centre possibly. Oh yes, lots of potential but, was it really coming up for sale?

And if it was, then could this scruffy girl he knew really have any sway with the owners? Of course not.

It was time for his viewing appointment. He painted a smile on his face, straightened his shoulders and strode off down the High Street where a young couple were waiting to be shown around a tiny flat in a converted house. It was shabby and old fashioned with a shared hallway and almost no sound proofing. It might be okay providing the guy upstairs didn't decide to go and have a pee. That had been the death knell to the last hopeful client. Apparently, the middle-aged lady who was downsizing after a divorce wasn't keen on listening to urine splashing into the toilet bowl just above her head, and to be honest, who could blame her?

Chapter 11

It was Monday. She hadn't come on Thursday or Friday and Jed spent the weekend worrying about his options. He would make an appointment to meet with the partners. He would tell them the owners of The Willows had decided to wait a while. He would say he was expecting to hear further. It was sort of true.

On Saturday afternoon he walked by the estate. The grand old gates were rusting in places and if part of Libby's work was to weed the front drive then she hadn't done a very good job. Still, if the owners were really intending to sell it was probably because money was short. Not many people could afford the costs of running such a place and it was not a surprise they were employing cheap casual staff, and it was no surprise that cheap casual staff didn't do a very good job.

It was a shame to see the place going downhill like this. Really it would be better if it was sold. It could be renovated and restored, and have a second life. Of course, the chances were, it would be demolished and forgotten. An estate of mock-Tudor houses would be thrown up with open plan front gardens and little metal weather vanes and faux stonework struggling to give the places an air of novelty and style.

He peered through the wrought iron bars and was gripped with a sort of zeal. If he could handle the sale, he would throw himself into it. He would do everything to find the perfect client, the best outcome for everyone. Then he remembered, it had been a casual comment from a girl who was at best flaky and there was probably nothing behind it.

He sat waiting for the bus on Monday morning with jitters in his stomach. If she came today, if she did, he would be sure not to upset her. He'd finesse her. He smiled at the word, it made him feel cunning and artful – just what people expected from estate agents after all. He'd pin her down, find out whether the projected sale was a real possibility. Maybe he wouldn't need Libby, perhaps it would be possible to make contact with the owners directly.

She didn't turn up and he sat on the number three gazing out of the window, rehearsing in his mind what he would say to Mr Bailey. He sighed, and as he did, he thought of Samantha and her comments. She was still being very cool with him. Property was such a small world – it didn't do to make enemies, and she was a rising star. He'd have to find a way to get back on her good side. Was it all worth it?

He wasn't convinced it was anymore.

Both partners were out for the morning, so he spent four hours in nervous torment. Molly had pencilled him in for two o'clock and he was torn between wanting to get on with it and wanting it to all go away.

"You got anything planned for lunchtime Samantha?"

"No." Though she was still speaking to him it wasn't the friendly banter they used to have. He would tell her what was going on. She'd come down on his side he was sure. She might even have some advice about what he could do. Being in the commercial section, there was no risk of her trying to whisk the deal out from under him.

"Fancy the pub?" He saw her hesitate. "Please."

She smiled and he saw her thaw.

"Okay. About half twelve?"

"Yeah, great."

* * *

"What would you like to drink, Sam?"

"A glass of Merlot would be great."

"There's a table in the corner, I'll bring the menu."

He ordered the drinks and leaned against the bar. The plasticised menu cards were in a stand nearby and he grabbed two. He was having a half of lager – his mind had to be sharp ready for the meeting.

"Hiya, wassup?" There she was, leaning against the chipped wooden counter grinning at him. She was wearing her usual denim and leather but her hair was tied in a pony tail on top of her head and she had a row of rings in one ear and a tiny skull and crossbones dangling from the other. A coloured scarf was wrapped around one wrist and there was a twined leather cord around her neck. She looked a little bit outrageous and very individual.

"Libby!"

"You not working then?"

"Yes, I am yes of course. It's lunchtime."

"Oh okay. You buyin'?"

"What – oh right – what do you want? Lager?" It was what she had drunk the last time.

"Yeah great." The barman served Jed's small glass and the red wine for Samantha.

"You with someone?"

"Can I get another lager please, a pint?" He turned back to her. "Yes – Samantha." He waved a hand towards the corner table where his colleague sat texting on her mobile. He was relieved that she hadn't seen him talking to Libby and then he felt a flush of shame. He turned back and watched in disbelief as Libby picked up the balloon glass of red wine, lifted it to her lips and drained it in three great gulps and slammed it back onto the bar top.

"Oooops, now your girlfriend's going to have to wait – sorry about that." She swung around and in a few swift strides was outside and gone.

"Oh, oh, woman trouble." The barman was grinning at him. "I guess you don't need the lager now?"

"What, oh er – no."

"Another wine?"

"Please."

"Can't live with 'em – can't shoot 'em." And with a short laugh the barman walked down the bar to pour another drink for Samantha.

* * *

I need to drink. I have had no food since the piece of toast which was brought and left by my bed before I woke. I thought earlier that someone was outside my door. I heard the rattle of the handle, but they didn't come in. It is an exquisite torture knowing that there is someone there. Do they know how it torments me? Are the footsteps, the occasional sounds of music and the slow opening of the door now and then deliberate means to distress me? If so, it works, and if not, then why don't they come in? What is the reason behind my solitude? Is it simply that I no longer matter, to anyone?

My glass is drained. I tipped it to my mouth and ran my finger around the bottom, there is not a drop left. It's strange but when I am thirsty and famished like this, things are clearer, my mind is sharper and the dizziness abates. Nature is cruel, one torment replaces another. I pray that they will come soon with just a drink. I think it is the same person each time now. I can't be sure but the shade and shape seems the same to me in my befuddled state. They seem sloppy, wearing one of those hooded tops. There is no need indoors to pull up a hood, it is sinister and unpleasant. Surely, they are not supposed to treat me like this? I haven't done anything wrong. Have I?

Chapter 12

Libby's behaviour threw him completely. He wandered back to the table in a state of total bewilderment. He had already accepted that she was unusual, but her action had been so spiteful and petty.

"So, are you going to come clean then? Tell me what happened in the interview." Samantha picked up her glass and sipped the wine.

"What? – Oh right. Well you've probably already got a good idea." She replaced the glass and leaned towards him. "I'm under the hammer – heh?" He tried for a laugh but knew it came out as pathetic.

"I'm sorry, Jed. Did they say when or anything?"

"No, not really. They just said that they didn't think I had – oh what was the word 'sparkled' that was it – apparently I haven't sparkled."

"Pillocks!"

"I don't know Sam, maybe they've got a point. I was so keen at the start, you know. I really wanted to do this, and I love the technical side, the surveying, the valuing, I really do but..." He stopped. "When you've shown people round as many cruddy properties as I have and seen their faces when what they see on the ground, compared to what they thought they were going to see…" She nodded at him and reached across the table and briefly laid a hand on top of his.

"Yes, I know – it's depressing."

"Too right. I almost feel like writing particulars that say stuff like: this flat is so small you won't have room for two chairs and a sofa if you seriously want to move around, and the windows are rotten under that new paint – oh you know – just honest. That way you wouldn't need to leave all the doors open to make the rooms look bigger, you wouldn't need to stand in front of the peeling paint in the kitchen and hope they don't want to look around on their own."

"I know but, Jed, it gets better. Anyway, that's been done before, the jokey 'honest' brochures and that should tell you something. Actually though, when you're showing someone around a lovely new apartment with all the fittings top line and their eyes are shining with excitement, it's a different thing."

"Yeah, I guess, but I haven't had the chance to do that yet and I just don't see how I ever am going to. Certainly not if they give me the boot."

"You know you haven't got the boot yet. Fight back, start to sparkle." She lifted her hands, fingers bent, and made the gesture of quotes.

Now was the time to tell her, to ask her what she thought would be the best way to handle the whole thing. Then he thought about Libby, odd little Libby and her peculiar behaviour just now, and handling The Willows seemed to be such an impossible idea that he decided not to bother.

"Have you heard of anything, on the grapevine? Anything that I might be able to have a punt at?" She shook her head. He knew anyway that if he was going to make this work it had to be by his own efforts.

They had their lunch and Jed did his best to be good company but it was obviously a struggle. As soon as they had finished eating, she glanced at her watch and made the transparent excuse of an appointment.

"Are we okay Sam? I'm sorry I upset you the other day. I was pretty brassed off to be honest and didn't want to talk about it."

"Yes, it's okay. Don't worry about it and you know what, Jed, at the end of the day if you do have to leave, there'll be other opportunities. It might turn out to be the best thing."

She was just being kind, but he smiled and nodded. They split up at the door of the pub and he slumped into the office to be told that the appointment had been cancelled because both partners had been called to a planning meeting.

Molly had pencilled him in for the next day, so he spent the afternoon making phone calls, chasing up reluctant viewers, touting for business and feeling thoroughly depressed.

Chapter 13

The clear autumn sun just didn't fit with his mood. As Jed plodded to the stop he moved under his own grey cloud of gloom. All night he had tossed and tangled under the duvet. His mum had been bright and cheery over breakfast. She had asked him about his plans, whether he had anything interesting happening, how sales were going. She asked about Samantha and Mr Bailey. It had been so hard to appear cheerful.

They had no idea that his job was on the line. As far as they were concerned, he was a success already. It just did not occur to either of his parents that he could possibly fail. He had done well at school, enjoyed his further studies, and had a job with an established and successful firm.

In their world, it was all very straightforward. He would step safely and surely up the ladder, until one day, he would either branch out to open his own business as his father had done, or buy into the partnership and sail towards retirement on the Good Ship Bailey and Herriot. The idea of coming home from work to tell them that he no longer had a job and his future was bleak made him feel physically sick.

It wasn't as if he could hide it for much longer either. It was only a question of time before Simon Bailey had the conversation with his father. How sorry they were, how it was really not Jed's fault, but he was a casualty of the financial climate. If things had been different, blah, blah, blah.

The early bus was vanishing into the distance as he plonked onto the seat. A group of senior students in the uniform of the local comprehensive were larking about on the opposite pavement. They looked so young and carefree. He wanted to back pedal and try again but he knew that now it was more a question of running to catch up with what he had allowed to drift away. He fiddled with his phone, checked his emails and then he heard the commotion.

Cat calls and whoops, it was the school kids of course, and he glanced up the road to where they were gathered in a group. They were hustling and pushing at each other, making obscene gestures and then from the middle of the group, her head high and looking as though she was completely unaware of their presence was Libby. She crossed the road without once glancing back and the boys were left looking stupid. They turned and headed off towards the school much quieter and just one of them glanced back and raised his hand, flipping the bird at Libby's retreating back.

"Wankers." She flopped on the seat next to him, totally unruffled, and pulled out the little box holding her joints.

"Yeah, idiots." Jed remembered being that age, doing such things and he felt ashamed. He gazed ahead and waited.

"So, how are you?" she asked.

He didn't know what he had expected, perhaps an apology, maybe an explanation. "I'm okay thanks – you?"

"Yeah." She carried on with the morning ritual.

"Yesterday, in the pub," he said, and waited for her to acknowledge that she understood, but there was nothing.

"I think you got the wrong end of the stick. Samantha, she's just a colleague."

The thing was, he didn't have any idea what she had thought. He had puzzled about it. She had called Samantha his girlfriend. Okay that was a mistake, but even if she had been what did it matter to Libby?

Libby turned to him. She tipped her head to one side, took a drag and coughed.

"Yeah well, sorry about yesterday. I was out of order."

It left him with nowhere to go. She had apologised, and there was nothing more to say. To pursue it now would make more of it than was reasonable and his mind was already racing down another avenue.

"Libby, you know the other day?"

She waited, just watched him.

"You said that you thought the people that own The Willows might be wanting to sell it?" He held his breath. Now was the moment she demurred, told him it wasn't true, it had been a mistake or perhaps she didn't even remember.

"Yeah right."

"Have you heard any more about that?"

"No."

"Oh, so it's not happening then?"

"Yeah it is, but no I haven't heard any more."

He turned and leaned towards her but backed off as the sweet smell of the marijuana tickled his nostrils.

"Okay, here's the thing. My job's on the line. It looks as though I might get the boot and…" he paused, gathering his thoughts. "The thing is that I may have given them a hint that The Willows is going to be up for sale and that maybe I could be in with a chance of handling it. Do you think – is there any possibility that you might be able to talk to somebody?"

"Oh, okay right. Yeah, I'll do that."

"Or I could come to the house. Maybe you could arrange for me to meet with them, the family." She shook her head.

"No, you can't do that. They're not there. They live abroad. It's all online, instructions and everything."

"Oh right. Do you have an email address for them then?"

"What do you need?" The question left him puzzled.

"Need?"

"Yeah to show your boss that you're going to be involved. What do you need?"

"Ideally, some sort of a letter, an appointment to do an inspection, something like that. Something in writing, best with my name on it, Carlisle, Jed Carlisle."

"Okay – here's your bus." She ground the end of the skinny joint under her boot, stood and swung away round the end of the shelter and headed back the way she had walked that morning.

* * *

I am stunned, I am shocked and delighted – I am delirious with joy. Sarah has been. Dear, dear Sarah, the door opened and there she was. Still so thin. "Hello Aunt Marian." That was all she said. It left me speechless. I pushed up to try to sit but the dizziness beat me back. "Don't get up. I can't stay long."

I gabbled at her, "I can't believe it, are you here, truly? I thought I was alone. We searched for so long, we tried and tried to find you. Come here, come closer."

"No, I have a cold – I don't want to give you germs."

"But I can hardly see you."

"It's alright, don't be upset. I'm back for a while. I can't stay just now but I will come back and we'll have a nice visit – soon." She raised a hand, blew me a kiss and then she was gone. It was so brief, fleeting and even now I can't believe that it wasn't a dream. After she had gone, I could smell her perfume, the girly flowery thing that she always wore.

Sarah has been, after all this time, all those tears. She has seen and she will surely help me. Oh, thank God.

Chapter 14

"Jed, good morning. Sorry about yesterday."

"It's fine Mr Bailey. Everything okay at the planning meeting?"

The man across the desk shrugged his expensively-suited shoulders.

"Planners, what can you say?"

Jed nodded, they shared the joke and the frustration. They were all in this together, except of course some of them were more *in* than others.

He took a deep breath. He couldn't believe the timing, yesterday he had dreaded this meeting but now…!

"If I may, first of all, I wanted to just touch base with you about The Willows." Bailey leaned forward imperceptibly, but the change in his demeanour pushed Jed on. "I have had a meeting with my contact." In the back of his mind a tiny red demon was laughing at the term *meeting;* he ignored it.

"Yes?"

"And I have things in place now to make contact with the owners. It seems that there is the distinct possibility that this is going to go ahead and that I, erm, we, are in at the beginning."

"Excellent, really first class. Well done. Now then, do you need any help? Would you like myself or Charles to sit in on your meetings?"

"I think at this point, sir, they want to keep things very low-key. I hope that's okay." Like a duck, paddling furiously under the surface but serene on top. His palms were sweating, he could feel the judder of his pulse in his neck. None of it was a lie, it was at worst an exaggeration, that was all, just estate agent speak.

"Yes, yes of course. The clients are the ones who must drive this. I would issue a little word of caution. I am sure, Jed, that there is no real need but I would be derelict in my duty if I didn't mention at this point that the main thing right now, up front, is to get something on paper. A contract if possible, an understanding of some sort – yes?"

"Oh yes of course, sir, of course. I will make that a priority. I think you should know that the owners are abroad. I am working now through my contact. I know that isn't ideal but…" He pursed his lips, left the phrase in the air.

"Hmm, no not ideal but, early days, eh Jed. Let's not get ahead of ourselves anyway. We have a long way to go before we pop the Champagne."

"Oh yes, sir, of course I realise that, but I just thought I would keep you updated."

"I appreciate that, Jed, I really do. Charles and I have had a chat. We are of the opinion that perhaps we didn't give enough consideration to how *invested* you were in your college work. We respect that and so, I do hope, Jed, that you didn't feel that the meeting we had a few days ago was too negative. It was more in the way of guidance. You do understand that, don't you?"

"Oh yes, sir, absolutely. I am grateful to you for being so honest. I am ready now to commit totally, and hopefully if this thing with The Willows comes together it will be the first of many."

"Let's hope so young man. Yes indeed. Let's hope so."

Jed took the stairs two at a time and gave a startled Samantha a thumbs up gesture as he hopped off the bottom step. He sat back behind his desk and logged on to his computer. Great, this was all great, it was all coming together. He pushed away the tiny worm of disquiet coiling and twisting in his gut.

Chapter 15

It was time to get things onto a more regulated footing. This was a multimillion pound deal and it had to be done right, properly handled.

Jed walked down to The Willows. The light was fading and there was a brittle chill in the air, but it wasn't unpleasant. He wasn't sure what he was going to do except that he harboured a small hope that he would spot Libby in the garden and they could have a talk. He needed names and details and most importantly he needed a signature somewhere, something concrete to move forward with.

The huge gates were closed. He was tempted to push them inwards over the weedy gravel and walk in. He peered through, skimmed his gaze back and forth, but the garden was empty. There were no exterior lights and nearer to the buildings at the end of the drive the shrubbery was a dark blur against the old stone. It was a beautiful building. What a thrill it would be to have a look around. He had always enjoyed that part of the job. Even inspecting the nasty little places had been interesting. He would walk around, mentally constructing particulars in his mind, putting a positive spin on old fireplaces – 'original features,' and tiny gardens – 'manageable outdoor living space'.

Yes, lately he had become disillusioned by the drudge of it but back in the day he had loved it. This would be different. Even if the place inside was decaying as much as the outside, it must still be pretty impressive and it wasn't dreadful, just a bit 'tired'. He wasn't expected and it would be bad form to simply turn up. Anyway, Libby said the owners were abroad and the place was fairly obviously deserted. That would put him in a difficult position if he went in and was caught on CCTV – unlikely but not impossible.

He would have to wait, pin Libby down the next time she joined him in the morning and move things along. She probably had no idea how it all worked, why should she? And she wouldn't understand the routine. He would push her to get permission to do the inspection as soon as possible and all his other work would be shuffled around to suit – this was the one, this was the deal that was going to make his name.

He walked alongside the stone wall, down the road and turned at the corner. Half way down the long run was a small wooden gate – a side entrance. Temptation overtook him and he grabbed the round iron handle and turned it. The gate swung inward smoothly and with two steps he was standing inside a small area of once cultivated garden. Gravel paths wound between the beds and, although much of the soil was bare and going over to weedy growth, he recognised some fruit bushes and an apple tree. Remains of the summer fruit were rotting on the ground.

The house door was a few metres away. It was partly glazed and had blue paint just beginning to fade on the lower half. He walked up to it and pressed his face against the glass. All he could see was a small utility room with a large Belfast sink and some shelves crowded with jars and pots. It was too dark to see further but he could make out some wellington boots and rain coats hanging from hooks on the wall.

It looked sad, harking back to the time when the house had been vigorous and active. Presumably this room had been used for handling and storing the produce from the plots around him. Beyond this must be the kitchen and he itched to look inside. He felt the same excitement he had felt five years ago when he had inspected his first few properties, before cynicism and disappointment had soured his enthusiasm.

He stepped away and went further into the grounds, but it was getting dark and there wasn't much point in hanging about. He spun in a circle taking in the declining grandeur and he grinned. This is what he had been hoping for all along and he blessed the luck that had brought Libby to him on a rain-swept morning just a few weeks ago.

He was careful to make sure the small gate was fully closed and secured, he rattled the handle and pushed at the wood and then marched back to the corner with descriptive phrases swirling in his mind. He would start drafting particulars tonight, just a few paragraphs about spacious grounds and imposing façades…

Chapter 16

"So, I saw you." Libby picked a stray piece of debris from the 'herbal' cigarette off her lip. She didn't look at him but swung her legs, kicking at the small stones under her feet.

"Sorry?"

"Last night. I saw you." She couldn't have seen him in the garden, there was no-one around, but then he thought perhaps she wasn't referring to his trespass. He had walked around the district and gone into The Feathers for a drink on his way home.

"Oh yeah. Where was that then?"

"At the house, The Willows. Is that what you do then? Snoop around to see if you like it?"

There was an edge to her voice, an undertone of ice he had never heard before. Yes, in the pub she had seemed spiteful and petty but this was something else.

"Oh, right. No not normally but I was at a loose end and I was erm, interested, curious. I just thought I'd pop down there and have a look through the gates and..." He shrugged his shoulders, gave her what he hoped was a self-deprecating smile.

"I couldn't resist. I was careful to lock it all up again afterwards. I just had a look at the garden. It's all part of the assessment process," he said. Perhaps he could befuddle her with verbiage. "A property of such importance, you know, it takes time to properly assess and estimate values and measurements and so on. I was just having a little look to get a better idea how we should present it to the market. Always providing of course that we are given the instruction."

"Or…" She turned to him now, looked him full in the face. "You just thought you'd come in and have a drool about it, nose around."

He twisted on the seat to look at her more directly, "I won't lie to you, Libby, I am excited about it. If we do handle this, it will be a huge thing for me. I don't suppose you have any idea how much a place like that is worth if it's offered to the right people. To make sure it makes as much as possible for the owners we have to plan. Okay you're right, I shouldn't have been in there, but I didn't think it would do any harm. Actually, I'm glad you brought it up because it would be really great if we could get things moving along, you know. It's coming up to winter and it's better to conduct viewings and things in the better weather."

"Yeah, okay. Thing is though, I live there."

"What?"

"Yeah, part of the job, I get to live there. There's a flat over the garage, that's where I stay so – somebody breaking in and prowling around…"

"Shit, Libby, I am sorry. If I'd known I would never have come in like that."

"Well now you do know, don't you? So next time tell me first."

"Of course, of course I will. Tell you what, can you give me your mobile number so I can call you?"

"No."

"Oh. Okay, what about a landline?"

"No."

"It's going to be a bit tricky. I mean we do need to have some contact. We'll need to arrange viewings and so on."

"I can see you here."

"Well – that's all a bit odd. Could we make appointments, time for you to come into the office?"

"No, I never know when I'm going to be free, that's not the way I roll. Here is all I can do. If it doesn't suit you just forget the whole thing."

"No, no we'll find a way round it. We'll manage it. First of all, though, I need an appointment to come and look round. To take measurements and photograph the rooms, all of that stuff, and I really need to have proper permission to do that. I could do with the address of the owners, their phone number – something."

"It's okay. When do you want to come?"

"No, I don't think you can give me that. It has to be from the owners. I need something in writing really. I have an agreement here in my case. Is there anyone who could sign that for me?"

"Yes, I'll get that done. I'll give it back to you in a few days, here."

She took the paper from him and rolled it into a tube. Gripping it in her left hand she stood up and walked away towards the newsagents.

As he climbed onto the bus Jed battled the unease he felt. This wasn't the way things were supposed to be done.

* * *

Sarah came again. She still has her cold, the poor love. She spoke to me from the chair beside the window. How I longed to touch her, to hold her. She is back in the area on business, she stays in a hotel. I would ask her to come and stay with me, but I don't want to frighten her away and I am in such a poor state. It is incredible that she has simply re-appeared, after all this time; I fear that I might wake and find it is a dream.

I asked about Elizabeth, but she wasn't forthcoming. She still appears to me so very young. Since we were last together, I have become a crone. My sight is fading, my strength is gone and yet she seems to have hardly aged at all. She wore a pair of trousers and a shirt and her hair pulled back from her face. I asked her to turn on the light, the better to see her but she thought the sudden brightness would be painful for me. Does she not understand that I would endure any discomfort to see her darling face more clearly? Maybe next time.

Apparently, there are papers from the solicitors for me. For so long I have given no thought to that side of life but yes, it must be done. She tells me they were found downstairs, overlooked by the agency people. She will bring them up to me next time.

Brief as they are her visits cheer me, but as she leaves the exhaustion overwhelms. She carried up my food, a sandwich and a drink, it was better than of late. Now that Sarah is here things must improve. I had no idea aging would be so very unpleasant — or so swift, for it seems to have come upon me unaccountably quickly. But then perhaps not, it's hard to follow the passing of time when so much of my life is wasted in sleep or in the horrible dizziness that has afflicted me.

Perhaps I should ask Sarah to call the doctor. I hate the thought of being prodded and mused over and I am afraid they will make me leave my home. I have heard that they have that power. The agency who sends my help promised they would do nothing regarding medical people without my consent, but it seems so very long since I have heard from them. The young supervisor who used to visit hasn't called for an age. I will speak to Sarah. They used to sit with me, talk to me and then they withdrew and the dizziness started and so I didn't look for company. It seems that it began quite suddenly and maybe it is a temporary affliction. Maybe one day I will wake and I will be myself again.

Chapter 17

"Hiya!"

"Morning, Libby." He had seen her walking towards him empty-handed and Jed struggled to keep his frustration under control. It was only yesterday he had given her the agreement. "How are you?"

"Yeah, I'm good." She settled in beside him and began her morning ritual. She glanced at him and grinned. He had an idea she was goading him, waiting for him to refer to her habit. He turned and peered up the road as if watching for the bus.

They sat for a few minutes in silence until she finished fiddling with Rizla papers and matches and then as the smoke swirled into the air around them, she mumbled, "How's it work then?"

"Huh, sorry?"

"This inspection, how do we arrange it? It will be with you, won't it?"

"Oh yes, yes it'll be me. So, what I'll do is come in and take some photographs. I'll measure the rooms and have a general look around. Then I'll do the outbuildings and the grounds. It'll take a while I expect – it's a big place."

"So, you have to go into all the rooms?" she asked.

"Yes, I do. I have to write the particulars and describe the condition and any special features, the views, mouldings in the plaster, original fireplaces, all that sort of thing. I'll probably dictate notes into my phone – that's my usual method anyway."

"And my place?"

"Sorry?"

"My place over the garage, it's just a little bedsit. You won't have to do that will you?"

"Oh erm, yes, I should do. It's all for sale after all, so yes, I should do. Is that a problem for you?"

She gazed at her feet swinging back and forth, trailing her toes on the gravelly pavement and scuffing up the toes of her battered boots. She reminded him of his sister when she had sulked as a child. "I'll try to be quick and not intrude too much. It's up to you how I do it. I can even come while you're out if you like."

"No. Not that, don't come if I'm not there." Her head shot up now and she looked him full in the face. "I have to be there."

Jed held up his hands, palms outwards towards her. "Okay, okay don't get upset."

She turned away again and took a big drag on the joint. "I'm responsible, you know. I'm supposed to make sure it's all okay. That's why I can live there."

"Yeah sure, of course. Don't worry I'll come when you're there and you can stick with me the whole time if you want to, but you know that's the whole point of the agreement. We take responsibility for what we're doing, did you not read it?"

"No, it wasn't for me was it?"

"Fair enough." Now that it was out there, he could ask her about it. "Have you any idea how long before I get it back?"

"Day after tomorrow maybe, maybe longer. I'm not sure. It went by courier but..." she gave a small shift of her shoulders.

"Great, that's great." The bus pulled into the stop with a hiss of brakes and the familiar thud of the automatic doors.

"See you tomorrow then?"

She didn't respond but simply tipped her head to one side and watched as he flashed his travel pass and wove up the aisle to his favourite seat near the back.

* * *

The office was quiet with most of the agents out working and Jed concentrated on his preliminary particulars. He was doing a general overview and needed to get a comment in about the sound of the river that he had heard from the garden. He knew it was close by, but if it was visible from the grounds that would be a huge plus. He wondered if there might be a private access or better still a small stretch that actually belonged to the property. He made a note to look that up at the Land Registry.

"Hey Dave, your girlfriend's back." Samantha called across the office to where the older man was busy typing. Jed spun to grin at her, detecting the note of teasing banter in her voice.

"Oh – has Dave got a lady friend?"

"Yes, there she is, out there. Been coming and gazing through the side window at us now and again for a few weeks now. Quick, look!" She pointed to the big window in the side of the building. It was almost completely obscured by notices and frames holding the photographs of houses and flats.

"You can't see her from there, quick come over here. I reckon she's got a thing about our Dave." Samantha picked up a jelly bean from the little bowl on her desk and flung it at Dave who was doing his best to ignore her. Jed strode around the corner of the office and leaned to peer between the posters. The figure was turning away. The dark jacket and mess of choppy hair was very familiar. He watched as Libby stepped into the road and jigged and dodged between the slowly moving traffic.

* * *

It has not been a good day. I have barely been able to keep my eyes open and when I do the nausea is overwhelming.

Sarah visited. She wanted to know why I hadn't eaten the soup that had been left on the tray by my bed. I told her that though it was a treat to have something hot, my stomach revolted at the thought of it. I heard her tut and felt so guilty, for I think it is her doing that my food is improving and so I pushed myself up and as she watched I spooned the lukewarm broth into my mouth. For a little while I did feel better but in no time at all the room was spinning and whirling and I had to ask her to leave. It broke my heart because my dearest wish is that she would stay.

I did manage to speak to her about having the doctor. She said that if I wish it then she will of course call him, but she feels that they will certainly insist that I go into hospital. I couldn't bear it, not as I feel now. She laughed at me when I told her I feel too ill to go to hospital.

We did manage to get the bit of business done. It was just a couple of documents to sign. She started to read them to me but it was about taxes and such and far too tedious and I simply asked for a pen and scrawled at the bottom of the pages where she showed me. I couldn't even make out my signature, though I did clasp her hand for a brief moment. I wanted to kiss it and to hold it to me, but I felt her stiffen. She never enjoyed physical contact, not since she was small. She never was one for cuddles. I want to touch her, wrap my arms around her but she keeps her distance and in the gloomy room without my glasses, all I see is the pale moon of her face. I let her go and when I woke again, I was in total darkness, another one of my days lost to sleep.

Chapter 18

Mr Bailey paused on his way through the office. "That matter we discussed, Jed, how is that coming along?"

"I'm working hard on it, Mr Bailey. I'm waiting for the agreement back from the owners and then I'll schedule the inspection."

"Excellent, first class. Don't forget, if I can be of any help just let me know."

"Yes, thanks – thanks very much."

He knew what would happen if he did call out for help. The partners would slide into negotiations and slowly and surreptitiously they would take over more and more of it. It wouldn't be a deliberate undermining of his position, but they wouldn't be able to keep their hands off it. He knew that he would be paid a reasonable commission, but he was determined to do it all himself. He would take it right through to completion. He would show them, show everyone, that he had what it takes to handle the good stuff.

It was Friday though, and he hadn't seen Libby since the glimpse of her dodging between the traffic. Now he would have to face the whole weekend waiting and wondering. He worked Saturdays, it was one of their busiest days, but his dad brought him in on his way to the Golf Club, and Sunday was a more casual day with just one or two of the agents working a rota. It would be Monday before there was any chance of moving forward.

She didn't have a phone – who didn't have a phone? How on earth could you function without one? He had three, one he used exclusively for work, a personal one and a spare just in case one of the others ran out of juice at the wrong time, and they always went flat just at the wrong time in his experience.

If he was to buy her one, would that give the wrong impression? It was so easy to step over the invisible lines that stretched around the business world. Would giving her a cheap phone so that he could contact her be seen as a bribe to make sure they were given the listing? The agreement for him to conduct the inspection was only the first step. After he had done that and written his report and crucially come up with his valuation, only then could they really begin to market the place. If he was going to have to wait days and days between each step, then it would take forever. Not only that, any delay left the way open for another agency to move in. The owners must be telling people about their plans and… okay they were abroad – he must find out where at the very least, he should have done that already. But word would spread and the vultures would descend and the only chance then of his firm holding on to the deal would be for the partners to handle it. So, the gift of a mobile phone – would that be unwise?

He couldn't ask for advice, if Simon Bailey were to find out that business was being conducted on such a casual basis, Jed would lose all credibility. Again, the little worm of disquiet nibbled at his gut. He wasn't sleeping, four times he had woken the night before with the 'what ifs' and 'maybes' churning in his mind.

* * *

When he saw her walking towards him on Monday morning with the brown envelope clutched in her hand, he had to fight back a strong urge to leap up and hug her. He had spent the weekend in apprehension. He'd been snappy and short-tempered, and the inevitable result had been a row with his father and a lonely session in The Feathers on Sunday evening.

"Hiya." She held out the envelope and then flopped onto the seat. He pulled the papers out a couple of inches and let them slide back down. He was itching to check the signature, but it would look unprofessional to drag them out here in the bus shelter in the fine drizzle. "All okay then?"

"Hmm, guess so," she said.

"Have you not looked at them?"

"Well – duh – no I put them in the envelope with my eyes closed."

"Oh yeah, of course. Sorry. So, when did you get them back?"

"Friday. They came by courier."

"Oh right. Where from?"

"What?"

"No, what I mean is where are the owners? Where did they have to come from?"

"Oh right. Yeah umm, Africa or somewhere like that. I just send them to a courier company."

"Oh – right. Blimey. Do they live there then?"

"Yeah, I think so, dunno."

She was lighting her spliff and peering up and down the road. Jed was frustrated by her attitude, but he had to handle her carefully. It would do no good to antagonise her again. He patted the envelope and turned to smile at her.

"Right, now I can organise the inspection. When would be a good time?"

"It's going to take a fair bit of time you said?"

"Oh yes, I think a good couple of hours."

"Not today then. Maybe tomorrow."

"In the morning?"

"Okay but not too early. About eleven-ish."

"Great, yep I can do that. Brilliant. So, I'll just come to the front gates then and you'll let me in?"

"No, come round the side. Where you were prowling about the other day. Come that way and I'll let you in through the kitchen."

"Oh, fair enough. I wasn't prowling."

"Yeah, it looked like prowling to me. So, once this is done what happens? How long is all this going to take?"

It struck him then that, with the sale, she would lose her job, and not only that, but her home as well. She had never mentioned that side of things and he had simply not given it any thought. He felt an unaccountable need to comfort and reassure her. "It will take a while. We will probably go to our own contacts first of all – with this sort of property we don't just stick a picture in the window, not straight away. We may eventually do that I expect but first of all we'll take it to people we know will be interested." She was nodding and looking forward across the road. He couldn't read her reaction.

"Then, there'll be viewings and offers and the searches and all of that, it takes quite a long time."

"Searches? What's that?"

"The solicitors have to make sure everything is in order legally, that whoever owns the property owns what they say they do. Oh yes, I need their names. So, I can put it in the paperwork."

"It's Carmody. Mrs Carmody."

"What's her first name? Does she own it totally, I mean there's no Mr Carmody or anything?" She just shrugged.

"I just call her Mrs Carmody when I email her, anyway you were telling me, what are the searches?"

"No problems, I can get it from the Land Registry."

"How do you do that then?"

"You just apply, the details for all properties are held there. You really haven't had anything to do with property sales have you?"

"No, why should I? When do you think I last sold a bloody house?"

"Sorry, yeah." He'd been thoughtless and a bit mean. He knew his life had been privileged and he tried to be kind when he dealt with other people who perhaps had struggled more. He felt ashamed for a minute as he looked at her in her scuffed shoes and tatty jacket. He'd buy her the phone.

"So, anyway the searches – they check boundaries and borders and rights of access, loads of things like that."

"But if you've done this viewing thing and you've got your agreement signed and everything, isn't that enough?"

"Oh no, blimey no. It's much more complicated than that."

"Oh right – it'll be a while then?" He was really sad for her but didn't know what to do or say. The number three swept down the road and squelched to a stop on the wet tarmac. He left her sitting in the damp morning gazing ahead knowing that she was going to lose her livelihood, her home and be forced to move on.

Why had he not seen this before? Obviously because he had been so caught up in the excitement of a huge deal, that's why. He felt dull and empty and really rather disgusted with himself. She had told him about the deal, she was helping him with it and at the end of the day she would be homeless, why? Why would she do that for someone she hardly knew – unless... Samantha's comments in the office came back to him, "I reckon she's got a thing about our Dave."

Libby had told him about it when he had said that he might lose his job, might have to move to London. Surely not! Surely this strange skinny girl wasn't trying to hold him just for the sake of a few minutes chat some mornings and the occasional, very occasional drink together. It didn't make sense because if her home was gone anyway... he shook his head and stared at his faint reflection in the grubby window. He pushed it away, if the place was for sale it was for sale, and someone had to handle it so why not him?

* * *

No Sarah today. Again, I found a meal beside my bed when I woke, some cheese and bread and a drink of fruit juice. I can hardly be bothered to eat but the empty pain in my belly forces me to chew and swallow. I enjoyed the drink though. It was a little warm and there was that rather unpleasant aftertaste, but the liquid felt good in my throat.

Someone opened my door and I called out to them to come in, please come in and talk to me, but there was no response. I heard music again from somewhere, I expect it was the cleaner from the agency. Are they still keeping the place nice? I have no way of knowing. Maybe they sit all day in the kitchen drinking tea. I will ask Sarah when she comes. I can't remember how long it is since I walked around my home, not since the dizziness first started at any rate.

I have been wandering in my mind, remembering the old days and the family before it fractured and fell apart. There is only Sarah now I think, oh yes and of course Elizabeth, but I haven't seen her since she was a tiny baby. I wonder how she has grown, whether she favours her mother or Brian. I don't expect I shall ever see her.

I don't know what I believe about an afterlife but maybe soon now I will join my sister and her husband, maybe they are truly all together in some blissful place waiting for me. How wonderful that will be, to see them all again, Mummy and Daddy and all the dogs and kittens and of course my beloved Edward and our poor dead baby. Rebecca – my daughter. If she had lived how different my life could be now. I would go now, right now if I had the wherewithal and to hell with those who would call me a sinner. What am I saying? There is no way for me to accomplish it, I am fated to slowly decay here in this room.

I pray that Sarah will come tomorrow.

Chapter 19

He couldn't sleep. It was ridiculous and he knew it, but he felt like a kid on Christmas Eve. He had looked over the documents from the Land Registry, he had his camera charged and the laser measuring device checked and ready.

The plans showed there was a part of the garden that led down to the river. A stretch of the bank and the water with fishing rights belonged to the house. There was a lake and about sixty acres of grounds, including what was shown as a small wood. It was even bigger than he had imagined. From the entrance it had looked substantial but there was no way to see the land that stretched to the river and then beyond.

He was quietly hoping that it wouldn't go to a developer. It was a beautiful property, and to see it turned into a cluster of houses would sadden him. He had to get the best deal he could though, and that was all there was to it. Of course, he would give the owners all the options, but his experience was that the amount of cash on offer was the deciding factor.

His first stop was going to be the hotel and conference centre developers. The partnership had a substantial list of people who might be interested and he would speak to

Simon and Charles about whom to approach first. He would have to refer to them at this stage because they had cultivated the standing relationships with the client base, but he would dig his heels in and be there at all the meetings. As he rolled about in his bed the thoughts whirled and spun; he was itching to get on with it.

* * *

It was a bright morning, a bit chilly but sunny. He had arranged to work from home to save travelling time and passed the first couple of hours checking and double checking his kit and getting rid of some of what he had come to think of now as, the dross. He completed details on one of the small flats and took an offer on a little terraced house which he passed on to the owners, and then handled the inevitable back and forth on the telephone – only for the whole thing to fall apart because of a difference of a couple of thousand pounds between the asking price and the offer. He flung his phone down on the desk in the home office in frustration.

Just after half past ten he left the house and walked slowly towards The Willows. He had dressed in his usual business clothes and carted his pilot's case with all his bits and pieces stowed inside.

When he reached the wooden gate, he paused. It felt ridiculous to knock when he had no idea whether or not there was anyone behind it, but after Libby's reaction last time he didn't want to walk in. Damn it, this was stupid. If she had a phone, he could just call her. He would go at the first opportunity and buy one and give it to her and tell her it was for her to use while they were doing the deal. He didn't want to offend her and would engineer it so that she believed it was a usual thing. Later it could all be forgotten and she could keep it.

He reached out towards the round iron handle, and as if she had been waiting for just that moment, Libby flung back the gate.

She was dressed in her normal casual manner but without the leather jacket. She had on a loose t-shirt and a necklace of beads and feathers dangled across her chest. He felt overdressed and faintly ridiculous and had to fight a strong urge to drag off his tie.

She stepped back to let him in and then turned to walk down the narrow pathway towards the half-glazed door. "Where do you want to start?" She was tense and the habitual playful grin was missing this morning. He remembered yesterday on the bus when he had realised for the first time the impact all of this would have on her. He would let her set the tone, and if she wanted it all done in a cold professional manner so be it.

"I'd like to start measuring and dictating at the front door, do the downstairs and then upper floors. Later I'll do the grounds and finally take pictures of everything."

"Some of it's a bit messy. It doesn't all get used."

"That's okay, I can deal with that."

He stepped into the utility room and she walked ahead of him through the kitchen and to the main part of the house. There was a narrow passageway which emerged from behind the grand staircase and then he was in a large square hallway. The flight of stairs was central, broad and imposing. At the first landing it split and the two flights that were formed turned back on themselves to serve left and right galleries overlooking the hall space.

Jed walked to the front door. Coloured glass panels sifted the light which pooled in blue and green sploshes on the old wooden floor. Though it was dusty and full of cobwebs it was beautiful and all that he had hoped it might be. Libby sat on the bottom step and leaned back with her elbows supporting her, obviously she was sticking with him. He smiled at her, a little embarrassed to have the audience as he began dictating into his phone.

* * *

There was some disturbance earlier today. I was awoken by the noise of the vacuum cleaner. It cheered me immensely. I believe this is more of dear Sarah's influence. For so long there has been silence and I imagined my home falling into filth and decay.

It is such a homely sound, that of someone carrying out the humdrum of housework. I wish they had pushed open the door and wheeled that noisy old machine around my space here. How normal that would have felt. I am pushed back in my mind to the summer when I had rheumatic fever and spent weeks in my room and how wonderful it was to have Rita come in with her lemon-scented polish for the wood and then the carpet sweeper rattling under my bed and around the chairs.

Now that I have no future, so much of my time is lived in the past and today has been one of memory upon memory and all the result of such an everyday occurrence.

I must have slept again. They have been in and cleaned around me, they have changed the bedding and I dreamt. I have struggled with beasts and Beelzebub. I was held and handled and abused. I have the impression of panic and of roughness. When I regained my senses, it was all made plain; they have been and washed me while I slept. The small bliss I had enjoyed earlier was ruined. It is unacceptable. It is the first time for a while that my passions have been so stirred but I am wrought with anger. The agency is paid to provide me with care and they are paid well. I have had no care, no compassion. They sneak and prowl and intrude when I am asleep. How it is accomplished without my waking I don't understand. It is as if I suffer under some outside influence, but I take nothing except my pain killers and they are here beside me on the table. It must stop. I will speak to Sarah and we will dismiss them.

Chapter 20

The interior of the main house was all he had imagined – spacious and gracious with floor to ceiling windows opening onto flagged patios. Ornate plasterwork, mahogany doors, balusters and banister rails. The main reception rooms on the ground floor were like something from the set of a costume drama. The kitchen had been refurbished and he was a little disappointed that it had been modernised.

There was a study to the right of the front door. Heavy drapes at the windows matched those in the sitting room but these had been pulled across the large windows. He dragged them back. A cloud of dust filled the air with sparkles in the low sunlight. Throughout the house the lovely old furniture was dusty and dull, so it would seem that Libby wasn't employed as cleaner or housekeeper. If she was, then she was falling down on the job.

Jed had his laser measurer ready to take dimensions but for a moment he stood and looked around. The floors were old polished boards with a carpet covering the centre. One wall had been lined with shelves and they were full of antique leather-bound books but there was a selection of modern paperback novels on the lower shelves. This wasn't a room caught in time – at least not until quite recently he thought. There was a gorgeous old fireplace with marble tiles and brass fender. The remains of the last fire were still there, dirty and disturbed by drafts and insects. He could imagine how it might have looked with the glow of the fire and the gentle light from the floor and desk light gleaming and reflecting from polished surfaces and glass and silver ornaments on the desk.

There were high-backed leather chairs pulled up before the hearth, attended with foot stools and side tables. A paperback was sitting on one of the little round tables and a bookmark poked out from between the pages. How very odd it seemed to leave a book half read and go off and travel abroad. He was struck by the thought that the story can't have been that good. He picked up the volume, it was poetry; ah well, that explained it then, he thought as he laid it back in the thin layer of dust.

He couldn't wait to begin taking the photographs. He knew that the flash would brighten the tops of the desk and side tables and bring the place to life. It was neglected but not to the extent that it would show in his images.

The dining room towards the rear of the hall, was wonderful – large and impressive, with French windows opening onto a terrace, and a view out toward a grassy expanse that sloped down to the banks of the river. He could see the willow trees that had given the estate its name, a line of them beside the lake, their branches swaying in the breeze. Further away the miniature woodland that he had seen on the plans glowed red and golden. The view from this room was magnificent.

The table in the centre of the room was huge, he estimated that it would seat twenty. There was a sideboard holding silverware, tarnished and sad. There were two crystal chandeliers, dusty and full of cobwebs, and everywhere had lost its brightness.

"Where next then?" Libby had hardly spoken to him, and it wasn't the way he had imagined this would be. She was quirky and prickly at times, but he had enjoyed their chats at the bus stop. They had laughed as they discussed topics in the news, the television or the other people passing. She was like a different person. Of course, now that the proceedings had begun, she had probably realised just how real it all was. He had come into contact with clients before who had backed out once they saw just what it was going to mean when they decided to sell their homes. People sometimes even changed their minds the night before they completed the deal, though that was thankfully pretty rare.

This wasn't her house, though somewhere in the grounds was her home, but he was surprised at the tension in the air. "Upstairs next. Are there any cellars?"

"One, but you get into it from outside."

"Right I'll do that later then." She turned and headed back to the hall.

He took some more pictures and sighed, she turned to him. "Wassup?"

"Oh nothing, I was just thinking about the history of the place. I don't suppose you know much about it do you?"

"Some."

"Oh really. Do you know the family?"

"I know they split up. They didn't look out for each other – not the way families should. Are you ready to go upstairs now?" She stomped to the staircase and stood to wait for him on the bottom step.

* * *

I thought I heard them but they didn't come to me, didn't bring me food or comfort of any sort. I dragged myself from my bed, to go to the door and call for them, to tell them to get out of my home and to leave me. Then I became afraid. If I do that, I will be alone and even the few steps I took exhausted me. I fell to the floor and crawled back like a dog and crept under the covers and I have cried but still the anger is there, seething.

The only blessing, and it is small, is that I do feel clean and the room smells fresher with new bedding and the commode emptied. I wanted to draw back those blessed curtains and throw the windows wide and breathe in the untainted air, but my strength failed me.

When Sarah comes again, we will talk this over and I will regain some control. I am so disturbed. For now, I will sleep, again I must sleep.

Chapter 21

This wasn't a stately home, the National Trust hadn't had their hands on it so there were no canopied beds in the upstairs rooms, no tapestry wall hangings, but there were paintings in heavy frames. He knew nothing about art but couldn't imagine that this house would hold worthless copies or cheap imitations. He didn't pay them too much mind, that was not his job, but he made a note to mention them to the auction department. Some had already gone, leaving pale squares on the walls, but maybe there would be more work to be had here and yet another feather for his cap.

The rooms were a good size with large windows, most had fireplaces and walk-in closets and the one at the front had an en-suite bathroom and dressing room. The furniture matched what he had already seen and though he would have loved to linger, gazing down to the river from this higher vantage point, he had to move on. The bathrooms were old fashioned and though there were four, on this level they had the air of disuse.

He had inspected seven of the eight rooms on the first floor. One more and then to the spaces that were in the roof. He expected they would be smaller and more in need of attention, but they were essential if the place was to be turned into a decent sized hotel. The downstairs rooms had to be gracious and impressive, but the guest rooms on the upper floor would increase the letting potential – providing they could be made into en-suite units and were large enough for a couple of twin beds and some storage.

He reached his hand to the last door on the left-hand landing. Locked. He turned to where Libby was standing leaning against the balcony rail. She nodded her head towards the door, "That one, it's locked."

"Oh. Don't you have the key then?" She shook her head and began to move away towards the narrow stairs in the corner. "Libby, hang on. I need to look at this room. It's the bigger one at the front isn't it, to match the one at the other side?"

"Dunno, never been in."

"Hell, this is a bit of a problem."

"Why?"

"Because I have to inspect it of course."

"Well you can't, can you? It's locked. Always has been. I dunno why. Not my business anyway. You'll have to guess."

"Guess?"

"Yeah, say it's like the other one only back to front."

"But Libby, that's not the way it works."

"Can't be helped. It's locked." Jed swallowed his disappointment; it wasn't her fault after all.

"If I can have the contact details for the owners then I can get in touch with them. I can ask for permission to have a locksmith open the door or perhaps someone has a key. Their solicitor maybe."

"Thing is, they want me to talk to you. They don't want to be bothered with it all, this viewing and stuff. They said they'll pay me if I deal with it all so I can't give you the contact stuff or I won't get paid."

"Shit, sorry – okay. Look, can you speak to them, ask them about this room? I really will need access. I can say in the particulars that it wasn't examined but when we do viewings we are going to need to get in there. Nobody is going to be interested in buying a place that they can't see. Then there will be surveyors and so on, they'll have to get in to make sure there are no structural problems."

"It's a bloody pain all this. I thought you'd just take a picture, stick it in the window and then someone would buy the place."

"Good God Libby, no. That's nothing like what happens." Her reaction was a sullen shrug and she turned and began to climb the steps.

"You'd better get it finished then. We still have the outside to do and my place and I'm gasping for a drink. I'll make us a coffee when we go to my place, yeah? This is boring."

"A coffee would be great, I'm sorry to put you out. I did say I could do it on my own though."

"No, it's my job. I need to be able to tell them I watched you."

So, she had a work ethic and moral code and maybe it wasn't part of her duties to keep the garden weeded and the furniture polished. The place wasn't actually filthy and there were no signs of mice or roaches and it was a huge place for one person to look after.

"Is there just you here, Libby?"

She spun to face him and peered down at him from the dimness of the upper landing.

"Course it is, how do you mean? Course it's just me."

"It just seems like a lot for you to look after on your own."

"Oh right, yeah well a bloke comes once a month to cut the grass. He used to do the garden properly but that's been stopped now. I guess they think there's no point if they're selling."

"Right, so you just check the security and so on do you?"

"Yeah and now and again I do a bit of cleaning, where it needs it. Nobody lives here, why would you need to clean it?"

He could have told her why, but it wasn't his business. However, he would suggest a team came in to smarten it up in preparation for viewings. It would all eventually be gutted, decorated and altered, but first impressions were still important.

He climbed into the attic rooms to find that in fact they were better than he had hoped with charming windows under the eaves looking to the river at the back and down the long drive and to the town at the front. He was ready for the coffee Libby had offered and then looking forward to a walk round the grounds and down to the lake.

* * *

No Sarah today and I did want to talk to her. This is all too much for me. I have calmed and thought things through and I am reaching a decision. I don't know how she will feel about it, with what happened before and the repercussions but maybe, just maybe, she could be persuaded to return. Oh not for all the time I know, she has her other life, but if I was to tell her that I will sign over the house to her straight away, make it hers, would she come and stay and let me see out my days here in comfort?

It may well be that she will refuse totally and I would understand. If that is the case then maybe the other solution would be to sell, to move into a – oh what do they call it – a facility. It appals me to even think of it but then I never imagined my life would end like this.

Chapter 22

The garage was a stone-built structure under tile; it was plenty big enough for three cars at least. Jed was surprised to see the blue Volkswagen Golf parked inside. He was still very much in the mood of the interior of the house and expected to have found a vintage car if anything, or at least something twenty or more years old slowly rusting away. This car was, in his estimation, only about eight years old. Like everything else it was covered in dust. "Is this yours then?" He called to Libby who turned to look at him from the top of the stairs where she was unlocking the door to her living space.

"Don't be stupid, do I look as though I drive around in a thing like that?"

"Sorry. Look, Libby, I know this is not very nice for you but there's no need to be so angry. I am trying my best here to be quick, but I have to do it right. I have to give it proper consideration." She peered down at him for a minute and then gave him a quick flash of her quirky grin.

"Yeah, sorry. I'm being a bitch, aren't I?"

"No, no I wouldn't say that, but you know I'm just doing my job."

"Okay, I know really. It's just odd that's all. I'm used to being on my own here and it's odd having someone else trailing around."

"Oh, thanks – I thought I was doing more than that."

"Well, you know what I mean. Come on, I've got coffee and I even bought a cake."

"You didn't need to do that. That's lovely."

"See, I'm not such a bitch after all eh. Listen, before we go in – you know, just – well it's my space."

"I'll be careful about what I photograph. Your house plants are none of my concern," he said. She grinned at him and gave a little shake of her head, he heard her giggle.

It was a small flat, everything pretty much in one area apart from the tiny bathroom. The kitchen was in an alcove off the lounge. It was okay, he'd seen much, much worse, but what impressed him really was that it was spotless. It was tidy and bright, there was a throw on the bed which looked Mexican or Indian, and there were beaded cushions piled against the headboard. She had two chairs facing each other either side of a coffee table. There was a breakfast bar where a vase of flowers was placed centrally. He could smell vanilla and noted the reed infusers in a clear glass bowl. He was intrigued. He had been into places before with marijuana growing, and the smell was unmistakable and at times overwhelming. So, where were they? He switched on the laser and measured the space, noted the view out towards the river in his dictation and then took a couple of pictures. She was grinning and he smiled back at her. He tried hard not to let her see him peeking into corners and behind the little dresser.

"D'ya really think I'm that stupid?" He shrugged his shoulders. "There's a greenhouse, it's pretty rotten but all the glass is still in there for now, I painted white over the windows and it's working well for the moment, till the weather goes colder. I think there's a heating system, but I haven't been able to sort it. Probably couldn't afford it anyway. I'll show you when we go into the garden." The atmosphere had lightened and as she brought the coffee mugs to the table he relaxed. The cake was good and they sat together and enjoyed the break.

"How did you get this job, Libby? Tell me to mind my own business if you like, but I just wondered how you would find this sort of thing."

"No, it's fine. I just saw an advert in the paper."

"Oh right, and do you like it?"

"It's something to do, somewhere to be." She glanced around and then repeated, "Somewhere to be."

"Don't you want to do something more though, you know, something with prospects."

"Prospects of what? Prospects of answering to some old fart in an office for years? Struggling to make money for someone else? Getting up in the morning and dashing for the bus in the rain." She stopped now and looked at him over the top of her mug.

"Fair enough. But after this, what will you do?"

"After this." She stopped for a while and considered. "After this it doesn't matter, anything else, anywhere else."

"What do you mean it doesn't matter?" But she stood now and picked up the two empty mugs and the plates and went into the little kitchen space. She rinsed them and left them on the draining board. "Come on then, I don't want to spend all day trailing round watching you take pictures."

* * *

Sarah came late. I had already slept of course but I could tell it was night. The darkness has another quality at night, deeper and more profound. She had been tied up with business she told me. I am not sure what she does but we always knew she would do well. Her degree was first class with honours and then she had so many offers of employment and even the chance to stay on and work for her doctorate. Her genius was flawed and how much better if we had realised the cost of such brilliance. Then, how much more would she have achieved if she hadn't met Brian? I try not to hate him, but when I think of the disaster that he brought to us, the pain and the horror... I would ask her what has become of him but I don't know how to. Is she alone now or is he there, prowling on the edge of our lives? I know that at first after she lost her parents, she was unreachable by those of us who wanted to help. He was the only one she wanted and so he had his way. All that anguish. Maybe now, at the eleventh hour, I can make some of it up to her.

Chapter 23

Meetings were arranged with several developers. Jed's estimate of six million pounds was agreed by the partners, but of course they would hope for a bidding war to take it higher if possible.

Now when Bailey or Herriot passed through the office they would stop and chat. The other agents had been tight-lipped about it all and he understood. Here he was, only just qualified and dragging himself back from the edge of dismissal and suddenly he was the 'blue-eyed boy'. He had heard via Samantha that a couple of them had decided it must be to do with his father, the old boy's network doing its stuff. It hurt his feelings and he'd tried to explain to her, but coming clean about the reality of the situation – chats at a bus stop and meetings in the street – was not the way to win kudos and engender confidence, so he just shrugged and carried on.

His pictures of the house and grounds were stunning and they had commissioned a helicopter pilot to do some aerial shots. Libby stuck with him for the whole of the four hours it had taken to do his inspection and they ended sitting beside the lake with a can of beer each.

The lake was man-made. It was fed from the river by means of a huge underground pipe, and then to avoid any flooding there was another massive drain downstream which was only partly hidden by a rise in the banks. This emptied back into the flow.

Jed had lived near the river all his life and knew that it was fast-flowing and dangerous in parts. They had always been warned to go only where inlets and pools had been cut to make safe areas but even then, swimming was discouraged. As they sat together on the rocks on the bank, he watched the swirls and eddies that spoke of hidden currents in the unexpectedly deep water. This lake hadn't been made to swim in; it had been made for the rearing and holding of fish. There were tanks at one side that could be closed with sliding gates. These were in a mess, the frames rusted and the concrete cracked and crumbling.

"There was some sort of accident here." The story had stirred deep in his memory.

"Hmm." She hardly seemed interested but he carried on.

"Yeah, way back, might have even been before I was born or anyway when I was really little. Some nutcase threw herself in, she drowned. There was more to it than that though. I'll ask my mum, she'll know."

"Yeah right, some story that everyone thinks they know."

He was stung and needed to come back at her with knowledge. "A couple of people died I know that much. We were always told not to swim in the river."

She pushed unexpectedly to her feet and dusted the bits of earth and grass from her skirt. "I've got to get on. Are you finished?"

"Yeah, yeah right. Sorry, I guess it was thoughtless of me to mention it, not very nice to think about really but, you know – it was so long ago." He shrugged as she turned away without another word and they climbed back up the lawn. He collected his bags and she saw him to the side gate with barely another word and he didn't know how to take his leave. If she had been one of his friends, he would have bent and given her a peck on the cheek but that didn't seem to fit with Libby and to shake hands seemed too cold and formal. In the end he turned through the gate and made do with a feeble wave which she didn't bother to return.

He promised to send a copy of the property particulars and a contract along with his report and valuation as soon as they were ready. Libby would use the courier again to forward them to the owners. Once they were approved and signed, he could really get on with the exciting part. He was itching to see the offers come in.

Back in the office the next day he kept his head down, he made coffee for a couple of the other agents, helped with their paperwork. He didn't like the feeling of being an odd one out.

The ordinary work still had to be done but he had rekindled his pleasure in the job and he wanted to fit in.

Things had changed though. Whether it was his more upbeat manner or an invisible aura of success that followed him, he'd moved three of his grim little properties in one day when a local landlord decided he could do them up cheaply and offer them as student lets.

He was heading back to work after signing the contracts when he saw her up ahead. There was something about the way the woman moved, the way that she held her head and swung her arms that was so familiar that he almost called out. But this couldn't be Libby. This woman was smart, her hair was pulled back from her face in a neat roll and, as she turned to glance up the road prior to crossing, he saw she wore a pair of oversized sunglasses against the low autumn sun. She was wearing a navy suit and low-heeled shoes and was so much the antithesis of the scruffy girl that he knew that the only conclusion was that this was Libby's doppelganger.

She had come out from one of the shops he passed on his way back to the office. Jed glanced into the window. It was an upmarket antique place and he knew the owner a little bit through his parent's dealings with him. As he passed, the old man was leaning into the window and waved at Jed who raised his hand in response. Good manners insisted that he should speak and he welcomed the excuse, so he pushed through the glazed door and heard the single chime of the old fashioned bell. "Hi, Mr Taylor, how's business?"

"Hello there, young man. Not too bad at all. How are your parents?"

"Fine thanks. Mr Taylor, you had a woman in here just a few minutes ago?"

"Ah yes, Miss Staple, charming young lady. A friend of yours, is she?"

"No, I thought it might have been an acquaintance really. Was she local, Miss erm, Staple?"

"No, I don't believe so, not any more. I understand she had family here but hasn't visited since she was much younger. She has had to come back to sort out her grandmother's estate."

"Oh right. I thought perhaps I'd met her somewhere."

"I understand she lived abroad until quite recently. We've had a couple of lovely little chats."

The feeling had started as a clutch in his gut and now moved up until he felt his throat tightening with nerves. He didn't want to ask but knew that he must.

"What did she bring, anything that Mum might be interested in?"

"Oh no bronzes I'm afraid, a nice little desk set today. It needs a polish but it's solid silver. Here, take a look. She has brought me some art as well and some jewellery, so sad clearing out but it has to be done." The old man shook his head and sighed.

He would have to check the pictures on his camera but he knew. As soon as he saw it, he knew that he had last seen this desk set in the faded study while carrying out the inspection of The Willows two days ago.

He tried to come up with a simple explanation. She was looking after the place after all. Perhaps she had been instructed to get rid of some articles before the sale. Perhaps that was a pig that had just flown overhead and was now roosting on the spire of the old church! His happy mood was soured and as he turned back into the street, he heard Mr Taylor calling after him, "Are you alright, Jed? You've gone terribly pale. You should go and get yourself a cup of tea." He raised his hand and trudged back to work.

* * *

These are long days when there is no Sarah. I detected sound and movement somewhere yesterday maybe, or the day before. The gardener I imagine. I have spent the days drifting, in and out of dreams and reminiscences, kind and cruel alike. Sometimes I just don't have the strength to fight and it is easier to float with my whirling brain into the past. They have been while I slept and left me food but I have spoken to no-one. I may as well be dead. Perhaps I am and this is hell; would hell be so very personal?

Chapter 24

He actually crossed his fingers. It was an unconscious move hidden under the desk as he clicked open the file folder and scrolled through to 'pictures'.

There it was though, crossed fingers or no, there on the lovely old desk was the tarnished tray, with its pen holder and inkwells. It gleamed in the reflection of the camera flash as he had known it would when he had angled the shot.

He sighed and closed the folder. He could ask her about it, outright and simple, the next time they met. He could write to her officially, but even as the thought flipped through his brain, he knew he wouldn't do that. What he couldn't do was ignore it, much as he would have liked to take that cowardly route.

The agreement to inspect the estate, and the contract to arrange the sale, were very clear – the agency were committed to taking care of the property while they were handling it. The clients they took around to view, any cleaning team they were to use, anyone who went in there under their auspices, were their responsibility and anything that went missing – well, it just couldn't happen. Things could not go missing, and here was proof that since he had been to the house the silver desk set had been taken away.

They weren't handling a sale of the goods and chattels, not yet at any rate, and so no official inventory had been done – but the house was effectively unoccupied and so if articles vanished there weren't many places to look for a culprit. Could he ask her? Well he didn't see how without inferring an accusation, upsetting her and maybe even losing the listing. She was after all the go-between in his dealings with the client.

He didn't know her situation, had no idea how she was fixed for money. Her clothes were simple, she didn't seem to have transport of her own and lived in one small space. If she was broke, then how tempting would it be to take advantage of the house sale? He didn't know what else if anything had been taken but there were the marks on the walls. The only thing that mattered right now though was the sterling silver and crystal that was in his photographs. It had been there when he toured the house, now it was in the shop round the corner.

It didn't matter that Mr Taylor would be more than ready to state where the goods had come from, rumour of malpractice would spread quickly and when it was thrown at a business that relied on goodwill to operate effectively then it just wasn't a risk anyone could take. An ugly and unfounded whisper could become an acknowledged fact all too easily. Speculation would be rife, did the agents know? Were they in league with the caretaker? Was it something they shared the proceeds of? He had asked Mr Taylor about her, what would the old man remember of that conversation? Perhaps just that he thought he knew her. It was a web all too ready to tangle. Either he called Libby out on it now or he fixed it himself. An idea slithered into his mind. He tossed it back and forth for a while, it might work. It could just save not only the reputation of the practice but his own as well.

He grabbed his jacket and hurried back to the main road. There was just time, it was half past four but if luck was with him the old man would be staying around until five. As he approached the shop, he was relieved to see the lights still burning inside.

"Hi, Mr Taylor, it's me, Jed."

"Oh, hello again, ah you look better now. A funny turn was it?"

"I was just hungry, I think. I've had a coffee and a biscuit and I'm fine now."

"Good, good. Now, what can I do for you?"

"That silver desk set you showed me earlier."

"Ah yes, a very pretty thing, dull and grubby but promising."

"I'd like to buy it please."

"Oh, really? I didn't think it was the sort of thing you youngsters were interested in. You're all computers and tablets and plastic nowadays."

"Yes, it's not for me. It's a little surprise present."

"Ah, not your mother's taste that, Jed. She's never been very interested in silver."

"No, my aunt. It's for my aunt."

"Ah, righty ho. Do you want me to get it cleaned up for you? I could have it ready for Monday."

"No, no that's fine. I'm not giving it to her right away, and it would just need cleaning again so I'll take it now."

"Hmm, it's a very old set. You won't go at it with the Brillo Pad now will you?"

"Oh no, of course not. I'll have it done professionally. I'll bring it back here actually, when it's time to give it to her."

"Oh, in that case why don't I just hang on to it? I can keep it in the strong room."

"No! Sorry no, that's fine – I – erm I want to show it to my cousin. Mr Taylor, we haven't discussed price." His fingers crossed again, he knew it was going to be expensive and he also knew just exactly how much was in his current account.

"I've had a good look at it and it's in perfect condition, not even a chip in the glass of the inkwells."

"Yes."

"I was thinking about one thousand two hundred pounds. It's a lovely example and the hallmarks are clear. It's bigger than many sets I have in, two inkwells, you normally only get that in a partner's set. I think maybe it was made to order originally, given time I could research it you know, it all adds to the value."

"Yes, yes – that's fine. That's good, I'll take it." The old man looked across the counter, his brow was furrowed, and he pursed his lips.

"As you wish then. I'll go and pop it in a box. I have to say though it's unusual to see you so enthusiastic, Jed, you have never shown much interest in your mother's collections."

"No, it's just that my aunt said recently how much she would like one and then I saw this and – as you say – it is lovely."

"Is this Daphne, your mother's sister? Lovely lady."

Shit.

"No, actually she isn't really my aunt, not a blood relation, you know. An old family friend and I've always called her aunt."

"Oh, not your godmother?"

Damn living in a small town and damn being in a well-known family in a small town.

"No, not her. Mr Taylor it's a surprise so…" He then appalled himself by tapping the side of his nose and winking.

"Ah – enough said, yes indeed. My lips are sealed." And with a knowing little chuckle the old man shuffled into his lair at the back of the shop.

By the time he arrived back in the office with the box under his arm most of the agents were packing up to leave, and Jed decided that he had just about had enough. What had started out as a good day with three contracts signed, had ended as a ludicrous exchange, and lie upon lie told to an old family friend.

Bloody Libby.

Chapter 25

His stomach clenched when he spotted her heading towards him. She swung along the road, head high, shoulders back. She had something about her, an air that she couldn't give a damn about anyone. Samantha was confident and self-assured, but Libby was something else.

Living in a small community had taught him to be careful about other people's opinions. A wrong word to one of the shopkeepers would get back to his parents and result in a row. When he first tried smoking, hiding in the park by the ancient bandstand it seemed that his mother knew about it before he had even finished coughing and puking into the bushes. He envied Libby her freedom. Okay it wouldn't suit him, her lonely life, but to be able to do what you liked, go where you wanted and not give a damn seemed so tempting now.

He had pushed the box into the back of his wardrobe. It would have to be returned to the house; but then what would happen if she saw it on the desk? He could stick it in a cupboard perhaps and then it would just seem to have been misplaced if the owners asked about it. How could he be with her though, knowing what he knew and unable to mention it? And what if she took more, what if she decided to slowly empty the house of all the valuable stuff? He needed to do something, but it had to be handled carefully.

"Y'alright." She flopped onto the seat beside him.

"Hello, yeah – you okay?"

"Yup."

"So, did you send off the contract and particulars?"

"I did, I said I would, and I did. God, nag, nag, nag."

"Sorry, didn't mean to nag. Just checking. So, we can do the inventory next then?"

"The what?"

"The inventory, you know, listing all the stuff that's inside." He waited for her to react, to tell him that she was acting for the owners, selling stuff.

"Why do you need to do that?"

"Oh, really just for security. We'll probably be sending in a cleaning crew. We mentioned that in the letter to the owners. We need to make sure we know just what's in there. It won't take long."

"I could do that for you."

"Uh?"

"If it's just a list of all the crap that's lying about, I could do that. It'd give me something to do anyway."

"No, I don't think that'll work. I think someone from the office has to be there, no offence and all but we are signing off on it."

"Right and you think I'll be pocketing the valuables?"

"No, no course not." His palms were sweating. "No, it's just another of those things, you know, it has to be done properly, legally." He was lying now and he felt the flush creep from his neck as his face grew hot.

"Well, please yourself." She took the wind out of his sails with the casual comment.

"Great, so when can I come and do it? This afternoon would be good for me."

"Bloody hell no, not this week at any rate."

"Okay, when then?"

"I don't know really, I've got stuff on. Anyway, until you get the paperwork back it doesn't really matter does it? I'll let you know. Here's your bus."

She crossed the road in front of the number three and without a backward glance she strode off towards the small row of shops.

That hadn't helped at all and he felt sick. Just when everything seemed to be going his way it had all soured again.

* * *

Sarah came and sat with me quietly this evening. I ate the scrambled eggs and toast that she brought in with her. For a little while I felt stronger, the food had bucked me up and I was able to sit against the pillows but in no time the dizziness afflicted me and I drifted in and out of my tortured sleep.

She didn't seem to mind. She spoke to me gently and I assume sat and waited while I slept. She wants to "fix" things for me, she said. Oh, what heaven to hear those words. I asked her what she would do. I was hoping against hope that she was planning to move in with me, but no. She said that she wants to get me strong enough to go outside. She is convinced that if I were to leave this room, I would regain my health. I have felt for some time that it may be the answer and I asked if she would draw back the drapes and open the window. Apparently, the weather is not conducive to such actions, a cold wind and rain in the air, and so she demurred but promised that soon she would arrange to take me outside. Perhaps a wheel chair, she says, out into the garden to sit on the terrace.

What a dream that would be, to see the garden again. I only wish my sight was not so faded nowadays, but I can sit and listen to the trees and I am sure that, in my poor befuddled mind, I will be able to see them.

We shall only be in the top of the grounds, I would ask her to take me no further, of course.

I have tried to remember when all this started. Until such a short time ago, I was aging of course but able to get about and to manage to make myself some small meals. The agency sent people to help with my bath because I was so afraid to fall again but I can't remember just when the dizziness started. Perhaps when the new girl came, ha, I use the term but I don't feel that she ever 'came', not really. I don't recall her name now and she has neglected me for certain, I don't think I ever actually met her. Certainly, she didn't help me to bathe but simply left food in the kitchen with a note and an excuse as to her early departures and late arrivals. I remember that the supervisor didn't come when she should and then it all becomes a blur, nausea, dizziness and confusion. I took to my bed and then this other person began to attend me, silent and rough.

I will ask Sarah to look around for another agency, or maybe if I regain enough strength, I will be able to handle things myself. We shall see, but there is light on my horizon – no, that's not it – there is light in my tunnel – that's sounds more correct. Yes, there is light in my tunnel.

Chapter 26

Jed clipped on his bow tie and heard his father huff as he came downstairs. "Honestly, Jed, I would have thought by now you'd have learned how to tie a proper dickie."

Jed wasn't in the mood for criticism, he wasn't in the mood for this bloody reception, but he hadn't been able to get out of it. Both partners would be there along with their wealthy developer clients. There had been no way to avoid it though. It was for a charity that his mother supported. Something for old codgers, that was what his father had said. It was really for carers and home help, in conjunction with a private agency, who worked with old people in the area who couldn't afford to pay for care. He sighed, turned around and summoned up a grin for his father watching from the bottom of the stairs.

"I know, Dad, I'm hopeless." He was rewarded with a smile and his dad threw an arm around his shoulders and shepherded him into the living room.

"Ah well, plenty of time I suppose, come on let's have a stiffener before we go and eat nasty little snacks and drink too much."

It wasn't that bad. A couple of his friends had been dragged along by their parents and they formed a little group near the end of the bar where they could watch what was going on and catch up.

"So, Jed, how are things at B and H these days?"

"Not too bad, Si, it's been quiet, but the signs are things are picking up now." He had been friendly with Simon Sharp since school, but hardly saw him now as he worked in London at an auction house.

"Are you handling anything decent yet, or have they still got you trying to shift nasty little bedsits and terraced junk?" There was no venom in the statement. Jed had spent drunken nights with Simon while they both complained about their lowly status in the business world. He couldn't help himself, though he knew it was small minded to brag, he really wanted to spread the good news among his peers.

"Yes, I still have my fair share of the grot Si, but between you and me I've just pulled off a bit of a coup."

"Oh right, what's that then?"

"Do you remember that estate – The Willows?"

"Yeah the one behind the long wall? It's got a river front hasn't it and a lake? Didn't someone drown there?"

"Yeah, I think so, way back. Anyway, I'm bringing it to the market."

"Oh, good man. The partners must be chuffed with you." Jed allowed a smile to smear across his face and then shrugged and lowered his gaze to the glass of wine in his hand. Perhaps he shouldn't have spoken but it felt good to impress his friend.

He felt a nudge in his back and turned to find his mother's friend Deidre, owner of the agency, leaning towards him. She laid a hand on his arm. "Did I hear you right, Jed, The Willows is being sold?" He glanced around and laid a finger on his lips.

"It's being kept a bit quiet for the moment Deidre. Mum's the word, yeah?"

"Of course, yes of course. I just wondered though, has Mrs Carmody died?"

"Mrs Carmody? Oh, you mean the owner? No I don't think so. They are still abroad though and they've decided to sell."

"Abroad?"

"Yes, is it Africa? I'm not sure."

"No, Mrs Carmody, the owner of The Willows." For a moment, neither of them spoke, both struggling to understand the other. "If the place is up for sale, I just thought maybe she'd died."

"No, I don't think anybody died. The family is abroad. There's a girl there, a caretaker sort of thing."

"Oh, that's very odd. That's really peculiar." The woman shook her head, causing the diamond drops in her ears to glint in the candlelight. "No, I mustn't start to gossip. I'm sure there is a perfectly simple explanation for all of it. I would be grateful though if you could let me know if you hear anything. I'm really surprised – gone abroad, huh." She turned and wandered off.

Jed's mind was spinning. He had to face it now – there was something off about all of this. He turned and scanned the room. As he did, Charles caught his eye and raised his wine glass in salute. He smiled back, and the swig of wine he took to settle his nerves tasted like vinegar in his mouth.

The name was the same, Carmody, but Deidre had been very confused. He wondered how much she would tell him if he called around to her office. Perhaps he could get some proper background. He had to admit though, that part of him didn't really want to know.

Chapter 27

It was payday and some of the money he had used to buy the desk set had been replaced. Jed walked into the phone shop and found the 'Pay As You Go' range.

"Can I help you mate?"

"I just want a cheap pay as you go. It's just for a sort of one off so I don't want anything clever."

"That can be false economy, you know. You think you don't want any bells and whistles but once you start to use it, you'll find it frustrating." Jed sighed. He had hoped to avoid this.

"To be honest mate, it's a present for someone but it's just short term, you know, so really I don't want to spend a lot."

"Right, well when you've decided, just bring it to the counter," said the assistant, who had already lost interest.

Once back in the office he charged up the handset and put on ten pounds in credit. He wrote the number on a piece of paper and entered it into his own smart phone. He had no idea what Libby's reaction was going to be, or how good she was with technology, so the simpler and more low-key the better.

He was on edge sitting at the stop the next morning; he had made the mistake of coming early again. It was stupid when the girl only ever turned up a few minutes before his bus was due. He had the box in his hands, turning it back and forth.

As usual, she flung herself down beside him, "Morning."

"Hi Libby, how are you?"

"Yeah – okay. You? Here's your papers and stuff." She handed him the large brown envelope.

"Brilliant, that's great. I'm glad I saw you actually."

"Yeah – I'll bet. You've been itching to get your hands on these haven't you?"

"Yes, course I have, thanks, but there's something else. I, erm, I wanted to ask you if you'd be okay to have this?" He handed her the box.

"What's this?"

"It's a mobile phone. We need to be able to contact you, now things are moving along. We need to call and arrange appointments or whatever. As you can't give us a land line number, we just thought this would be the best option. You can keep it until after the sale and then if you want you can give it back to us, or not, it can be written off as an expense." He dragged the piece of paper from his pocket. "I wrote the number down and it's already charged and has some credit on it." As he spoke, she stood and turned. She held the box at arm's length pushing it towards him.

"No, I don't want this."

"It's just to make things easier Libby. To be honest it's really a pain that I can't call you, and I can only see you in the morning when you come here or if I bump into you in town. It's just not the way to do things. Apart from anything else it's causing me problems at work because I'm having to stay quiet about how we're doing this."

"Tough. If you can't hack it then maybe I should find someone who can."

"Libby, wait." She spun away and took a step towards the kerb. He reached out and grabbed at her arm. "Wait, look, you have to do these things properly. What do you think the owners would say if they knew you were being so difficult? They've given you the job of handling this and you can't do a good job if it's not even possible to phone you." She turned back, her eyes blazed and when she spoke it was a hiss, low and unpleasant.

"Listen, I don't have to do what you want, I don't have to do what the family want, I don't have to do anything anyone else tells me to do. I make my own way, I make my own decisions, and if I choose not to be available to you twenty-four seven then you will have to deal with it."

She thrust the box at him. He had no choice but to let go of her and use both hands to catch it before it slipped to the floor.

"Libby, you're overreacting. Look, if you like we'll agree times when we can call, something like that, just once a day?"

"I said no." She stormed into the traffic and dodged and wove her way to the other side of the road, and then disappeared down a narrow alley between two of the shops.

Jed flopped back onto the seat muttering under his breath, "Bloody hell, what was that all about?" He was unnerved by her reaction and the recurrent feeling that this thing was about to come tumbling down round his ears, and that everything, including his future at the office, was built of straw and could be blown away in a moment.

* * *

Sarah's talk of taking me outside took root in my mind. I couldn't shift it, my every waking moment, though there were few to be sure, the idea nibbled and picked at my brain until I could bear it no longer. I can't estimate how long I have been in this room, how many hours I have spent in this bed, wasting the countable numbers of days left of my life in dizziness and sleep and so I decided that I must act.

It seemed to me that the longer I lay there static and still, the more my body would waste away and degenerate, so I forced myself to move.

It was so difficult, my legs could hardly bear my slight weight. They quivered and shook, and as I pushed from the bed I clutched and grabbed at the things around me. I was afraid I may fall again as I did at the start of all of this. With my diminishing vision I had to move slowly lest I collide with the dresser, the stool, the wardrobe. The things that once I knew so well have become a threat but I did it. I made it to the window and dragged and pulled at the heavy drapes. They had been closed for so long that they had forgotten how to slide; how ridiculous that such a small thing as pulling back my curtains should exhaust me, but in truth after the first one opened I had to sink to the floor to catch my breath and fight against the dizziness. That was a mistake of course and for a while I thought I would never be able to regain my feet, and how embarrassing to be found slumped in the corner of the room should Sarah come.

I rolled to my knees and by dragging and pulling on the edge of the dressing table and the wall for support I managed, but I was so weakened by the effort that there was no pleasure in my victory. I staggered back to bed and fell onto the covers and rather than a smile of joy at the extra light, I found tears tracking across my face and the darkness came and took me away.

When I woke it cheered me to see the brightness, and the shadowed shapes of my furniture, and a little colour. The accomplishment gave me strength to leave the bed again and I was overtaken with a sort of mad compulsion and I turned to the door. I would go and open the door and then insist that it be left open. I would become part of the world again, listen to the sounds of the house, small though they might be and hear the clock in the hall and maybe the clatter of the cleaners.

I was suddenly angry for allowing myself to be cut off so. I should have insisted that the room be left open all along. But what use is anger now in the face of my discovery? I leaned on the bed and the ottoman and then launched myself like a new born calf. My hand still had the memory of where the knob was, and I confess that I had to pause a moment before I swept it wide to re-enter my home. How foolish I feel now, how saddened and yes, afraid, for my door is locked. I am imprisoned.

Chapter 28

The contract had been returned and everything was in place. In the office it was all coming to a head. Viewings were arranged and Jed was making spreadsheets and timesheets, organising refreshments and cleaners. Charles insisted on being kept up to date at every stage and called on the intercom repeatedly asking for times and dates. It was one of the biggest deals to come along for years and the partners were twitchy and anxious.

"Come along now, Jed, move this along. With a bit of a push we should have some real action by the end of this week. I have to say I'm looking forward to seeing the place myself. You won't mind if I tag along now will you? Just as an observer of course."

"No, no of course, sir, that's fine. Thing is though, there's a problem with the phones." Not a total lie. "I need to arrange for the gates to be opened and the doors unlocked. Will it be okay if I pop out of the office? It might be best if I jog along there and have a word in person?"

"Off you go young man."

"Right, right. I shouldn't be more than an hour or so."

It was time for him to take the reigns. He didn't work for bloody Libby, Bailey and Herriot were under contract to the owners of the property. All this messing about and hysteria was nothing more than Libby trying to put off the sale. He could understand it; she would lose her job and her home. He thought that probably she had been told to get things moving some time ago, and when he met her at the bus stop that very first day it hadn't been the happy accident it seemed. Not for her anyway and maybe – and it galled him to realise this – maybe she thought he was such small fry that it would actually delay things rather than progress them.

He had thought about it endlessly and remembered the day she had been seen looking through the office window. Samantha said she'd done it a few times. Of course, it all made sense now. She had been sussing it all out, and then she had engineered the bus stop meeting. After all, if she had really been taking her job seriously, she should have been in town, going around the agencies and trying to set things up.

He went directly to the small side gate and pushed it open. "Libby, you there?" There was no sign of life as he walked through the kitchen garden. The small blue door was locked and so he turned and followed the path round to the front of the building. He rang the bell but couldn't hear it sounding in the house. He hammered on the wood and waited before thumping a second time, still nothing.

By the time he had reached the garage, his irritation was building. This was a ridiculous waste of time. If she had taken the phone, he could have done his job so easily and efficiently. He banged on her front door and shouted her name and still there was no answer. So, she must be out in the town and he was faced with going back to the office with nothing resolved, unless she was down in the greenhouse with the plants. He had nothing to lose and so clattered back down the stairs and across the lawn but even before he reached the shabby old building, it was obvious it was empty. Damn it. He glanced at his watch. He had been out of the office just over three quarters of an hour and could risk a bit longer waiting. He would go back to the front of the house and then he would spot her no matter which gate she used, because she would have to pass him to get to her bedsit.

He headed across the expanse of lawn, striding out in frustration. He glanced towards the river and the gracious sway of the great willows slowed him. It was a gorgeous spot. He turned and headed downwards now to walk around the lake, a couple of minutes in the quiet would calm him a bit.

He nearly missed her, in dark clothes among the shadows and crouched low on the rocks she was almost invisible. His first reaction was relief. He could talk to her after all. He quickened his step. As he came nearer something in her attitude slowed him again. She was curled on a flat boulder with legs drawn up and her face buried in her hands. Her shoulders were hunched and he saw them heave and understood that she was alone in the garden, crying beside the lake.

He was lost and had no idea what to do. He had never seen her like this. The Libby he knew was bright, confident and cocky – or just lately, fuming with anger. It was a shock seeing her like this, so obviously in despair. And he shouldn't have been there anyway. "Shit." He swung his head back and forth. Should he sneak back the way he had come and wait at the house, or man up and approach her? His instinct was to go down and just wrap his arms round her. He was surprised by how much it hurt him to see her like this. He wanted to just go and give her a hug. If he did that though, then he couldn't exactly bring up the subject of viewings and contacts and all that stuff. All he would be able to do was hold her and try to make her feel better. Whatever it was that was causing her upset, surely a warm hug and a friendly shoulder would help.

He shook his head, turned on his heel and climbed up
the lawn, he glanced back once to see her still sitting on
the rocks, alone. He went into the office and told them
that it hadn't been possible to finalise the arrangements
after all, but it would be done for sure the next day and
everything was under control.

Chapter 29

Jed didn't go into the office the next morning; he spent an hour working on his computer at home. At ten he pulled on his suit jacket and walked down to The Willows. He didn't allow any time for hesitation but pushed open the side gate, crossed the front of the house and thumped up the stairs on the side of the garage block.

He knocked and waited, listening for sounds of life inside. There were none. As he turned to descend the flight of wooden steps Libby was coming towards him across the grass.

"Oh, it's you." She didn't climb the steps but stayed at the base looking up. "I wondered where you were." She was carrying a thin plastic carrier bag and was obviously coming back from her morning walk.

"Yes, I needed to see you, to speak to you. We have to arrange access for the viewings."

"Right – what about that other thing?"

"What thing?"

"Counting the teaspoons or whatever?" Once he had bought it and sneaked it back into the house, hiding it in the sideboard, he had forgotten the lie about doing an inventory, trying to shock her into discussing the desk set.

In his mind the thing had been dealt with. If he hadn't been so stressed, he would have handled that better.

"Oh yeah, we might not have to do that now. We've got a few people interested already so it might move even more quickly than we thought."

She looked away, glancing to the river. "So, how long do you think then?"

"Depends, if we can do the viewings this week, Friday or Saturday, then we can ask for sealed bids by the end of next week or the beginning of the week after."

"What's that?"

"When we have a property like this, with a few people interested they have to submit their bids. They are kept secret and then when we open them, we pick the best offer. They all have an idea of how much we are hoping for and it's up to them to put a proposal together that beats everyone else's."

"Bloody hell it's complicated."

"No, it's not, not really, actually it's quite exciting and it means that we don't have so much bother with people who are just nosey parkers and time wasters. Anyway, the thing now is to do the viewings. You don't have to be here if you don't want."

"I'll be here. I'll keep out of the way, but I'll be here."

"So, it'll be Friday, I hope that's okay. Can you make sure the gates are open?"

"Yup. Friday."

"I'll drop a letter in with a note of the times and so on."

"Fine. Do you want a cup of coffee?"

"No, it's fine. I have to get to work, get everything sorted."

"Suit yourself." He brushed past her at the bottom of the stairs and with just a small wave he walked back to the kitchen garden and on out into the road. He had to keep her at arm's length, above all he couldn't get involved with her – that way lay disaster and he wasn't going to risk everything now for the sake of a prickly, moody girl who would be moving on soon anyway. He pushed away the vision of her curled on a rock beside the water.

* * *

I tried to stay awake, I tried so very hard but it is beyond me. Oh, where is Sarah, does she know? She can't possibly, she would surely be as appalled as I to know that the door is locked. But how is it that she doesn't know? Do they know when she is coming? Do they run and turn the key when they hear her car? I have never heard a car but I suppose that is not surprising. She must come down the drive and then as they see her, they unlock my door and pretend that all is in order. That is what they do, wicked, wicked — they have no right to do this, and what is the purpose? They know I am ill, they know I can't see. Ah, wait, is that it, are they worried that I may walk out and fall down the stairs as I did before? Of course, oh stupid old woman that I am, they mean to help me, to protect me or maybe to protect themselves, the agency would be responsible were I to fall. Nonetheless I shan't have it, I won't allow it.

I have slept again and I have missed them. I tried to hold on, to speak to whoever brought my drink and the dull sandwich but yet again they came and went without me knowing. They have drawn the curtains. I cried when I saw, all that effort and for just a short hour or so of precious light and now I am plunged back into the dark.

I hope that Sarah comes soon, it seems so long since she has been but time is confused for me, hours are endless, perhaps it is not so long after all. It seems so very long though. They have kept me cleaner of late, it is done while I am sleeping but a blessing for all that. The room is fresher than for a while and I have clean bedding most days. If only they would open the windows.

Chapter 30

Jed had searched the paperwork from the brown envelope, he had gone through his own copies and then done it all again, but what he was looking for just wasn't there.

He had asked for permission to enter the locked room, suggesting a locksmith come and carefully open the door in the event that the current owners didn't know where the key was. It had been a separate letter with a place for them to sign their agreement.

It wasn't there.

Could he act without it? He knew that their usual locksmith wouldn't work without the paperwork – it was more than his reputation was worth.

He had to go and speak to Libby again. He should have done this on the last visit. This should have been sorted before now but he'd screwed up again.

Perhaps she had sorted the documents and mislaid this one.

Once the office was closed, he grabbed a quick sandwich and a pint and caught the later bus home. He stayed on until the stop after his usual one because it took him nearer to The Willows' side gate.

As he climbed the steps beside the garage, he could hear music from inside the little unit and saw a light from behind thin curtains.

She opened the door quickly after his knock and stood in the doorway looking at him without a word. "Hi Libby, it's about Friday, or the viewing generally really." She nodded, she didn't invite him in, but kept her hand on the door frame, arm braced across it. He detected the sweet smell of her pot. "I'm really sorry to disturb you but there's a letter missing from the package and I wondered if you knew anything about it." Still she didn't speak but merely cocked her head to one side. "You know that locked room? The one upstairs at the front? I asked the owners for permission to go in there, and that document isn't in the envelope."

She shrugged.

"Thing is I can't do the viewings with the room inaccessible and I can't have the locksmith open it without permission."

"Right. What do you want me to do?" She wasn't exactly unfriendly but unhelpful and taciturn.

"Well, did you take any of the papers out? I thought maybe they had been separated." She was shaking her head before he finished speaking.

"Didn't take 'em out. No need was there."

"Shit, this is a bit of a bugger isn't it? Look, I need you to ring them, it's urgent. Ask them if they can send something by email or fax – or let me do it. Let me contact them."

Again, she shook her head. "They're away. I don't ring them, no phone remember?" She raised her eyebrows. "It's all online, emails or letter by the courier."

"Yes, but you have their contact details."

"No, I mean they're away from their usual place. On holiday or something I reckon. Out of touch for a while. I had an email just saying to let them know after everyone had been."

"You've got to be kidding me."

"Nothing I can do – sorry." She began to push the door closed.

"Okay, okay look, you're the caretaker. Let's do it like this. You sign the permission and be there when we open the door and make sure we don't damage anything and then I can write to the owners and tell them what's happened. That's probably going to be okay. You are in charge after all."

"No bloody way. I don't know why that room's locked do I? Could be the crown jewels in there, no, sorry."

"Right, fine, email them though, would you? Try your best, give it a go. Just do that, okay?"

He spun away from her and stomped down the stairs. She called after him, "Still see you Friday, will I?"

"Yes."

* * *

What is this place? How is it that I am here? It's cold and this bed, this narrow bed, is not mine. The dark here is deeper than in my room. Total. Unless I am blind now. I fear I have lost what little there was left of my sight. Oh, someone help me.

What is this new horror?

I don't know where I am.

There is a smell, from the past – a cold dead smell, the scent of rot and damp.

It can't be. Can it be? I am in the cellar.

No.

Oh think, think. I had my meal, my drink, I was in my room. The nausea began again and I lay on my pillow. Nothing after that. No journey, no visits, nothing.

Am I dead then? Is this it? A lonely eternity in a place that terrified me as a child.

Help me someone. Please.

Chapter 31

The weather was horrible, cold and wet. Jed had checked and the forecast for Friday was better, he certainly hoped so. If the clients could see the house and especially the gardens in the sunshine it would be a big plus. It would put everyone in a good mood and show the place at its best. He pulled out his smartphone and swiped through to the Met Office site again. Nothing had changed, he slipped it back into his pocket and glanced around.

The bus was late. He spotted Libby striding down the pavement, head up as usual, oblivious to her soaked hair trailing in rat's tails across her face and dripping onto the black leather of her short jacket.

She came to a halt in front of him, forcing him to tip his head back to look into her face. "Thought I'd missed you. Door's open."

"What?"

"That door, it's open."

He jumped to his feet, his instinct was to reach out and hug her, but as usual he had to curb his natural tactile nature. "Brilliant. That's excellent – how come?"

She shrugged, "Key came in the post, nowhere else it could have been for really, was there? I went in and opened the room."

"What's in there?"

"Same as the other pretty much. Bed, wardrobe, the usual stuff. It was niffy though. I opened the window and – you know – cleaned it up a bit."

"Oh, thanks Libby. The cleaners are coming later this morning anyway but thanks so much."

"Yeah well, as I say it was a bit rank in there so… Anyway just thought I'd let you know. See you tomorrow." And with that she turned and stalked off back the way she had come.

He felt his face lifting in a grin. He'd buy her something, chocolates or – no – beer, he'd buy her some beer to say thank you. It wasn't that she had done much really. The key had come because he had insisted she contact the owners, which was her job but she had gone in and cleaned it she said, and then come to let him know. Yes, some beer or wine.

Seven developers had signed up for viewing. It was by invitation only, the shiny brochures had been sent out and now with this excellent news, everything was looking good.

God, he was nervous.

* * *

I have never felt such pain. There isn't a part of my body that doesn't ache. I can see a little now, grey shapes and dark walls but that is all and I am so cold. I have curled under the cover and shivered for hours.

I want this all to end, I can't take any more.

I tried earlier to walk and to find the door but I had to give it up after a few steps. There is nothing for me to cling to and I am like a babe on shaking legs.

I can see this place in memory. The stone shelves and the flags on the floor, the moisture that dripped in the corners and the sacks that held potatoes and turnips. They are probably long gone now though; we haven't used it for years.

I was small when Estelle locked me in here, we both were. She always maintained that it was accidental, I don't know — I have never known. Was that a precursor to her looming problems? Perhaps so. I was lost for hours and I remember my mother's tears when they found me. They told me later that she had run around the lake screaming my name, convinced that I had drowned. How ironic. Poor Estelle.

I could never come into this place since that day and now here I am. I have cried, of course I have, but what is the use? There is evil at work that is clear and I have played it back in my mind, the events that brought me to this.

When the agency girls first came, they were kind and they took care of me very well. Then I found the note telling me that the staff had changed. I was stupid, I should have made enquiries. I should have demanded an explanation, but I was so tired and my ankle was sore after the fall, I needed pills for the pain. That was when the dizziness began. The nausea and the retreat to my room and the lack of food, of care. But I haven't taken the tablets for such a long time now, I can't blame those for my continued infirmity.

There is no excuse, I have let things slide, I've brought this trouble on myself by relying on others and now I reap the rewards but why? Who? And what am I to do? I must move. If I can move, then I will be warmer.

I could give up now, lay in this cold, damp place and I know that I won't last long, I am old and sick. Or I can fight, move and shout and try to draw attention to my plight if I have the heart.

I will sleep for a little. I will sleep and when I wake then I'll move and fight, later. Afterwards.

Chapter 32

"You're in a good mood this morning." Jed's mum smiled up into his face. He had jogged down the stairs and swept her up in his arms.

"Yeah well, it's today."

"Oh, I know that, of course I do. I am excited for you, dear. I hope it goes really, really well and then they all get into a bidding war and the whole thing exceeds anything you have expected."

"To be honest I'm so nervous just now, I'll be relieved if I don't fall down the stairs and make an idiot of myself."

"Don't be silly, you'll be great and then tonight we'll have a glass of champagne and go out to Mario's to celebrate."

"Brilliant."

She stretched up onto her tiptoes and kissed his cheek. "We are very proud of you. Come on, get on with your muesli or you'll be late and that wouldn't be what you want. I'm giving you a lift in today aren't I?"

"Oh yeah, that would be great. I don't want to rely on the bus today of all days, it's bound to be late, or break down or something."

"Come on then, let's get going."

Charles Herriot turned his Bentley in between the iron gates and swept down the drive. "It certainly is an impressive property, Jed. Well it has been, and I am sure it could be again."

"Yes, I have to admit that I hope someone takes it on who doesn't want to demolish and put up some new build units."

"Indeed, anyway, we will see. I think planning permission could be a problem with the river so close. People are very worried about flooding these days but let's not get ahead of ourselves. Come on, we just have time for a quick walk through before the first of the clients arrive."

As they climbed up the broad steps, Jed glanced around, looking for Libby. She had said that she would keep out of the way and he really hoped she had meant it. He hated feeling like this about her but couldn't be sure just how she would behave in front of the rich developers who were about to descend on The Willows.

The cleaners had been in, and though the job they had done was fairly superficial the place looked good and smelled clean and fresh. There were vases of flowers on tables and they had found towels and linens to make up the beds and equip the bathrooms. As he approached the second bedroom in the front of the house, Jed wished he'd had a chance to double check that it was actually open, but as he reached down to the brass handle and turned it, he felt the lock click smoothly.

Inside it looked no different from the other bedrooms. The walls were covered with old fashioned rose-decked paper and the furniture was similar to that in the rest of the house. He noticed that the windows had been left open in this room allowing the cool breeze in, so obviously the cleaners had felt the same as Libby that it had needed airing.

The first of the cars arrived and they went back down the grand staircase to get to work and as they did Jed's phone chirruped in his pocket. He glanced at Charles who raised his eyebrows at the oversight. "You'd better answer that and then turn the darned thing off."

"Yes, sorry – it is my business line and it's the office." He received a curt nod in response. "Hi."

"Oh, hi Jed, it's Molly."

"Hello Moll. We are about to start the viewings."

"I know, sorry – I have had a call from Irwin's Solicitors – Mr Irwin himself rang the office. He wants to speak to you. He said it's about The Willows. He acts for the owners he said, and it's fairly urgent. He asked if you could call in when you've finished there. He's in the office all day and he's asked to be informed as soon as you arrive."

"Right. He didn't give you any other idea of what it's about then?"

"No – he did ask me to contact you straight away. I wouldn't have called otherwise – I know it's a big day and all that."

"It's fine. Thanks Molly." He powered down the handset and slipped it into his pocket.

It was probably nothing, some little glitch with the paperwork that's all, really it was probably nothing.

He tried to swallow the dry lump that had formed in his throat and stretch his mouth into a grin.

He looked across the lawn and spotted a dark figure moving over the grass and disappearing into the disreputable greenhouse. He hoped Libby had remembered that she had promised to hide her plants for the day.

"It's going well, Jed?"

"Yes, they seem pretty impressed, don't they?"

"They do indeed, now then, where are the keys to the cellar? We need to have a look in there, did you bring a torch – or perhaps there is light down there?"

"No, there's no electric, I have my torch in my bag, but it's not locked."

"Yes, yes it is. We've been down there and it's inaccessible."

"Oh, it wasn't last time I was here." As he spoke the truth hit him like a blow to the back of the head. Stupid Libby, she'd stuck her plants down there and then locked the bloody door.

"Hmm, sorry sir, but I don't have a key – it must be with the caretaker, and as far as I know she's not available today."

"Hmm – bit of a slip up there, Jed, it would have been better to have her around. No matter, I'll put them off for now."

He turned away with a grimace. Far better to let him think he had cocked it up than have them walk into a cannabis farm – wasn't it?

Chapter 33

"Sorry to have to bring you in, Jed, but I really am so snowed under. I couldn't get away from the office today."

"It's fine, Mr Irwin. I was just coming back from The Willows anyway."

"Ah yes, viewings today I think?"

Jed nodded, *come on get on with it.*

"And how was Mrs Carmody?"

"I'm sorry, I don't know what you mean. We didn't see her, she's not there."

"Ah – right, that was why I needed to speak to you. I have been trying to contact her." The solicitor leaned back and folded his hands across his chest. Now he was ready to get on with what he had really wanted to say. "I have to admit that I was surprised to receive the paperwork from your office. I can't claim that we have acted often for the family recently, but over the years we have been involved with their legal business, and I would have expected that she would have let us know that the property was to come to the market. I wondered if we had done something to offend her, so…" Here he just raised his hands palms upwards and paused, obviously Jed was supposed to say something.

"Sorry, but I don't know anything about that, Mr Irwin. I have never met her myself of course. Your practice was named on the documents and so we sent you courtesy copies."

"You've never met her?"

"No."

"But, then how are you receiving her instructions?"

At the bus stop, from a difficult young woman who smokes pot and bites my head off on a regular basis.

"I have a contact, the caretaker at the property and they have asked her to deal with me directly."

"But who is this caretaker? Do you mean the helpers from the care agency?"

"No, it's a young woman, living in the apartment above the garage. She's there on her own."

"But, in that case where is Mrs Carmody? I have tried to contact her, I telephoned but imagined that the number we have is out of date when there was no answer. I did drive around there a couple of times but found no-one at home."

"No, I believe she's still away, I think it's Africa, isn't it?"

"Away – Mrs Carmody? Well, this is very confusing, Jed, very confusing indeed. Mrs Carmody has been in poor health for a while to my certain knowledge. She has always been quite a solitary soul anyway, since her sister and brother-in-law died so tragically, and," he waved a hand in the air, "all that awful business with her niece. I find it very difficult to believe that she is 'away' as you say."

Jed shrugged his shoulders. He had no response.

Irwin pulled out the file. "These copies of your instructions, they are genuine I suppose?"

"Genuine, yes of course. I'm not sure what you mean."

"Hmm, the signature seems to match those we have on record, a little shakier perhaps but that's to be expected as she must be quite old now." He peered at the papers on his desk and shook his head. "I'm uneasy, Jed, I am very uneasy. Perhaps you could ask this caretaker person to see me. I would like to set my own mind at rest. I find it very difficult to believe that our client has gone anywhere at all – let alone abroad – it just seems so unlikely. Of course, people change, and I haven't seen her for a couple of years but still…"

"I'll speak to Libby; I'll see if I can arrange something, but in the meantime do you see any reason why we shouldn't carry on with the sale? We are asking for sealed bids by a week next Wednesday."

"Right, of course I can't expect you to act on the strength of my 'feelings', so I suppose you must carry on. Please, Jed, I would ask you as a personal favour to try to have this woman come in to see me or at the very least give us a number so that I can speak directly to Mrs Carmody."

He wasn't going to get into the 'no phones only email' conversation just now, he just couldn't face it. It had been a day of such highs and then finishing on a low – he was mentally frazzled.

He went to the off licence and bought a six pack of lager. He would go in the morning and see Libby. Surely there must be a way to speak to this mysterious Mrs Carmody, someone must have her number or Libby would just have to ask for it. She needed to explain, he would write the email for her. As the thought passed through his mind it was followed with the vision of her at the bus stop when he had tried to give her the phone. Hmm, perhaps there was another way.

The thing was underway now, rolling on and from the point of view of Bailey and Herriot it was all just a case of making as much money as possible on the deal. Surely there was no way for it to go wrong. The papers had been signed and witnessed, so okay he hadn't seen that happen, how could he when they had been thousands of miles away? Perhaps, after all he should have been up front with Charles and Simon. He should have told them the exact situation; perhaps he should have looked for their approval of the way he was handling things.

Who was he kidding? No-one in their right minds would approve of what he had done, it was flaky at best.

Tomorrow he would be stronger, he would get it all on a proper footing and then he could enjoy the bids and the finalising of the deal. No more pussyfooting around.

Chapter 34

"What's this for?" Libby pointed at the pack of lager.

"It's, you know, just to say thanks for your help." Jed walked into the room and deposited the beer on the floor, near the pedal bin.

"It went well yesterday. I should think we'll get some good bids." She didn't answer but moved to the sink and began to fill the kettle.

"Coffee?"

"Thanks, yeah."

Once the drink was made, they moved outside and sat on the top step in a patch of weak sunshine.

"Did you shift the plants out of the cellar? I was grateful to you for moving them, but now a couple of people want to come back and just see that last place."

"Cellar?"

"Yeah."

"Nope, not me. I put the plants over in the woods. I put some old wood planks over them, polythene. Cellar would have been too cold. The woods were too cold really but no, not me."

"Have you got the key?" She pursed her lips and shook her head.

"Can I see your keys, Libby?" He expected an explosion of anger or an out and out refusal but she uncurled from her seat and leaned inside the door. The bunch of keys hanging on the hook wasn't as big as he would have expected, just five keys and a leather fob. She handed them over and then bent to pick up their empty cups.

"This is the one for the house, yeah?" She stood beside him and reached out for the ring.

"House, main gate, my place, the one for that bedroom, it doesn't fit any of the others, bit odd that but," she shrugged "and that's for the garage main door."

"The cellar door was locked yesterday."

"Do you want to go and see now?" She was in a really good mood. It was odd but he would make the most of it.

"Yeah, if you don't mind." He was even more surprised when she reached out and laid a hand on his arm.

"I've been a bit of a bitch, I know, stuff on my mind. Sorry." And with that she turned away and jogged down the flight of concrete stairs.

* * *

Jed rattled and shook the old wooden door. He had wondered if it was just swollen with damp but that didn't seem to be the case. It moved in the frame but wouldn't open. Libby stood at the top of the four steps with her arms wrapped around herself. He turned back and shook his head.

"Any ideas?" He heard her sigh and as she turned away, she called to him over her shoulder.

"Come back to my place. We need to talk."

Inside the little bedsit was as clean and neat as on his first visit, no matter what else, she was particular about her living space. She pointed to one of the chairs and flopped down in the other.

"Okay, look, I need to tell you something but don't let on – yeah?"

"Okay."

"I got this job on the understanding that I'd be here to look after the place. Thing is though, the pay is crap, I mean really bad. They take the rent out of my wage and it means that they're not even paying me the minimum. I have to pay my own bills, electric and so on, and it makes things really tight. I have some debts, other stuff." This wasn't what he had been expecting but as she leaned towards him Jed didn't interrupt. "So, I've got another job, it's in one of the shops, up by the bus stop. It's cash in hand, just for a few hours a day in the stock room and it really helps out. Course it means that I'm not here all the time, not like I'm supposed to be, so…"

"Right, I see, so what you're saying is that things might happen here and you wouldn't know about it."

"Pretty much, yeah. I think that someone else comes sometimes. It's just a feeling but now and then it feels – oh I don't know – disturbed. If you tell anyone I might lose the job. Okay, I know I'm going to lose it anyway, but I was hoping I'd have a bit of time. So, I guess that's it. Although, not quite it, there's another thing." She stopped, considered, and then shook her head, "it doesn't matter, we all have stuff, don't we?" For a moment he felt a like a wimp as he thought back and tried to find some 'stuff' in his past but he knew instinctively she wasn't talking about pinching jelly worms from the Pick & Mix at Tesco.

"Don't worry, Libby. I won't tell anyone. It doesn't make any difference to me really, although it does mean that the place isn't that secure doesn't it?" In the back of his mind was the desk set, and her comment about debts. He couldn't ask, not now that she had confided in him, not with the re-warming of their relationship.

"Do you think that whoever is coming in could have locked the cellar? Why though, why would anyone do that? It doesn't make sense." She shook her head.

"I don't know, all I know really is that I didn't lock it."

"Bloody hell, what's this all about? Look there's something else, the solicitor who will handle the legal side of things…" Jed paused, he was nervous, but maybe with her in this new mood it could be easier than he had imagined. "He's a bit bothered about the fact that I haven't ever met the owner, and, well just the way I've handled things. He asked if you'd go in and see him."

"Me – why?"

"Actually, to be honest I don't really know now you mention it but, would you? He wants to ask about the contact details and so on." Her answer took him by surprise.

"Oh, okay then. I'm handling this though, you know, that hasn't changed. Anyway, they're away. Last time I was in touch, it's only on the internet, emails, PMs, that sort of thing, anyway, she said they were going to a place where there'd be no Wi-Fi, nothing, it must be really isolated, I didn't know there were such places, but hey what do I know?"

"If you just tell him that and then it's up to him, I guess."

"Right, will you arrange it?"

"I will, thanks Libby."

She leaned to the coffee table and opened the little wooden box that was in the middle. She lifted out a spliff and waved it at him. She grinned as he nodded just once and then lifted the plastic disposable lighter and held the flame to the twist of paper.

* * *

Has she gone, oh has she? Is it too late? Sarah, was that you? Did you not hear me?

Chapter 35

"Jed, phone for you – Mr Irwin."

"Thanks, Molly. Good morning, Mr Irwin, how are you?"

"Fine thank you. I have just had a word with Miss Carlton."

"Oh right, good." At least she had turned up.

"I have to say that it all seems rather odd, but she has put my mind at rest somewhat. She brought with her a contract of employment for her position as caretaker at The Willows."

"Oh right, good."

"She refused to give me any contact details though, Jed; she is a very determined young woman, isn't she?" Was that a note of admiration he heard in the solicitor's tone?

"Yes, yes she can be."

"It seems that she is unwilling to give me email or Skype addresses as she has been tasked with the running of the property and the progress of this sale. She did also point out that if Mrs Carmody had wanted me to be able to contact her, she would have made sure I knew how." Jed was convinced he heard a chuckle. "Well, that did rather put me in my place! No matter, she has agreed to let our client know that I would like to have a word and we have left it at that. I have to say I was impressed by her attitude; it is rare these days to find someone so committed to following instructions. So, we will see what happens next."

"Right, good. So, we'll just continue then, shall we?"

"I don't see any reason why not." Jed replaced the receiver and lowered himself to his chair.

"You okay, Jed?"

"What, oh yeah fine, just had a surprise that's all."

"In a good way?"

"Yes – it's fine, Molly, thanks."

* * *

All seven developers had submitted bids and the envelopes had been locked in the safe until the deadline. Now it was here. They were making quite a thing of it; champagne had been poured and the senior staff had gathered in the conference room. There were big grins all round and as Charles handed Jed the first envelope a flutter of excitement spread through the room.

It was brilliant. They had all come up to the suggested asking price and three had gone beyond it. There was even a smatter of applause as the last envelope was opened and Jed felt his face burn.

Now it was time to go through the bids carefully and find the one that had the best chance of going all the way to completion. The partners took their seats and began reading the reams of documentation.

It was a result, a real result and though he tried to behave professionally Jed felt his face creasing in a grin. He looked up and Charles winked at him – Charles actually winked at him!

* * *

As he opened the side gate, Jed had very mixed feelings. Yes, he was flushed with success, everyone was delighted. They had spent the last few days in conversation with lawyers and money men, pushing the planning department to come back with their thoughts and the developers themselves. In the end The Willows was probably going to become a boutique hotel, spa and conference centre. Charles had been right about the Planning Department and building new homes so near the river. Nobody thought that would be approved, and so the old house would be saved, changed yes, but the essence would remain.

He had brought the paperwork for Libby to send on to the client for approval. As far as he knew contact was still limited and Irwin's were very twitchy about not being able to speak directly to Mrs Carmody, but it seemed that there was nothing to be done about it. He was surprised to find her in the vegetable garden. She was pulling the last few apples from one of the trees.

"Oh hiya."

"Alright. Do you want an apple?" She tossed one of the fruits to him, but he was off guard with his briefcase in one hand and the other still on the gate, so it crashed to the floor at his feet splitting on the old flags.

"Butterfingers." She laughed. "D'ya want coffee?"

"Yeah, great. I've got some papers for you to send on. Are you in touch with them? Everybody is itching to get on with it now," he said.

"Yeah, I had an email yesterday. They wanted to know if I'd heard anything."

"Brilliant."

They moved into the bedsit and she bustled about with the kettle and mugs. "Libby, did the surveyors get into the cellar the other day?"

"Nope, wanted to take a crow bar to the door, didn't they? I told 'em to bugger off."

"Right, of course it's not a deal breaker, nobody seems to think it'll be a problem. According to the plans it's only a little space and doesn't impact on the foundations or anything."

"Right, so is that it then? All sorted?"

"Pretty much, if the owners are happy. Look, Libby, I do know that this complicates things for you and I just want to say that if there is anything I can do to help, you know, find you a new place or whatever…"

"Thanks. Really thanks, that's nice. I'm not sure what I'm doing after this though."

* * *

I don't want to open my eyes. I don't want to be here and yet I know I am. I am so cold, this blanket is damp, everything is damp. I cough continually and someone has sneaked in while I was, well what? Not sleeping. It's not sleep but a stupor. They left a tiny light and a bottle of water; it is no comfort to me.

My only comfort now will come when I die. Sarah has run off yet again, it must be so or surely she would have searched, she would have torn the place apart to find me. Unless they have lied to her, perhaps they have told her I am ill, in hospital. I fear not though. My heart is broken and I don't understand why. I am alone and I want to die and now at last the dizziness and nausea that have been my constant companions are abating – how cruel are the gods.

Chapter 36

"Come on, old woman, open your eyes."

"What is this? Who is this? Let me be. Sarah – Sarah is that you?"

"Sit up, come on sit up. You have to sign this."

"Leave me be, leave me alone. I am in pain."

"Pain? You have no idea about pain. You old witch, sign this paper and let's be finished with this."

"What is it, what is that?"

"It's the end, that's what it is."

"The end of what? Oh, leave me. Sarah, I can't see you – what is this all about?"

"It's about justice, you old bat. Justice and – yes – revenge."

"Help me, please take me back into my room. I'm ill, I can't breathe properly. Please, Sarah, help me."

"Your room. Help you. You can't breathe. It's all about you isn't it – always has been, all about you. Nobody helped me, nobody gave me a room when I was destitute and miles from home. Nobody cared when I was ill and nearly died. Nobody helped when I had to raise my child on my own. Nobody cared when Brian had gone and then she left me as well and I was alone."

"Sarah, Sarah, I don't know what you're talking about. What are you talking about?"

"No, you wouldn't know, would you? You wouldn't know because you never cared. You never tried to find out, did you?"

"Sarah, I don't understand. I thought you'd come home. I thought we were family again."

"Family? Don't make me laugh. What would you know about family?"

"Oh Sarah, don't, don't, you're hurting my arm. You are all I have left. Don't do this."

"No, you evil old bugger, I'm not all you have left. You have nothing left. Nothing – do you understand? You are going to sign this paper and then you truly will have nothing."

"What is it? If I sign it will you help me, will you get me the doctor? Here, let me sign it, if you will just take me back to my room. There, there it's done. Sarah, no, don't leave me, don't lock me in, Sarah. Please, come back – please."

* * *

"Libby, hey what's up?" Jed had glanced up from his desk to see the girl at the window staring in at him.

"D'ya want to come for a drink?"

He glanced at his watch, "Okay, give me five minutes. I'll see you in the pub ..."

"Are you okay, Libby? You looked a bit worried before."

"Did I? No, I'm fine. Well, to be honest I'm just feeling a bit down."

"That doesn't seem to be like you, the way you normally seem to me, I mean."

"Hmm, sometimes there's just stuff isn't there," she said.

"What sort of stuff?"

"You know just stuff."

"Do you want to talk about it? With me I mean."

"Tell you what, why don't you come over tonight. We can hang at my place. I'll make some food. I'm not going to have the flat for much longer, it'll be good to have a visitor."

"That'd be great, really. I'd like that. Do you want me to bring something?"

"Well, you could bring something to drink if you like but you know, Jed, I won't be making quails' eggs or whatever else it is that your mum makes."

"Don't be silly, anything'll be great."

"Right, cool."

He walked back to the office with a big grin on his face. Maybe things were moving along, if he could persuade her to relax with him, let him get to know her a bit then maybe their friendship would stand a chance of becoming something more – special."

* * *

The Lord is my shepherd, I shall not want, he leadeth me beside the still water. Still water. Beside the still water. I need water.

Chapter 37

"I brought some beer and some red wine. I wasn't sure what'd go with what you were making."

"I made a chilli so whatever you like, I guess. Let's have a beer first though eh? We can sit in the garden and watch the sun go down."

Jed was pleased by her mellow mood, she had been very subdued earlier, and now she was herself again. She smiled as she passed a bowl of tortilla chips and a glass for his drink.

"There y'go, you take those and I'll bring a blanket. The grass is a bit wet."

Of course, it could be the marijuana. He wondered again whether or not she used anything else. It scared him to think that she may fall victim to the modern scourge. He pushed the thoughts away, it was none of his business after all.

"You seem a bit better, Libby."

"Yeah sorry about before, I was a bit fed up."

"Do you want to talk about it?"

"No, no it's fine. I'm fine."

"Okay, if you're sure. Can I ask you though, about you? I don't know anything about you. You just turned up at the bus stop."

"There's nothing to tell. I mean what sort of thing do you want to know?" She had laid back on the blanket now and was gazing up at the darkening sky. He'd never seen her so relaxed.

"Where are you from, Libby? You never mention your family. Do they live near?"

"No, I never see them. My mum's a nutcase."

He burst out laughing, "Come on, don't be silly. We all think that about our parents at times, that and more besides."

"No, Jed. She is; she's really ill. She was in hospital, over and over when I was a kid."

"Oh, oh I'm sorry. I thought you were just, you know, using the term to mean…" he shrugged.

"Yeah, I know, but unfortunately in my case it's actually true. My mum is totally nuts. It runs in the family, apparently."

"But, you're okay."

"Am I? You don't know. You don't really know me. I could be a raving axe murderer. How would you know?"

"Well, the axe might be a giveaway." In spite of herself Libby laughed.

"Yeah, I guess. No, listen. My grandmother was what they referred to as delicate, highly strung. That was the start of the problems. My mum – nobody even thought about her, when she was young. They were always too busy trying to protect Estelle, her mother. This is just what I've been told. I never knew any of my relatives."

"Okay."

"Anyway, my mum got pregnant, she wasn't married."

"You." He raised his finger and pointed at her, she nodded.

"My dad, he was okay my dad, but he wasn't good enough, not for the posh family that my mum comes from. They wanted her to have an abortion." She stopped for a moment. "That would have been that wouldn't it? Probably better all round."

"Don't say that, Libby. Please don't."

"Well, whatever. My mum wouldn't and there was a row. A humdinger of a row apparently, went on for days and then –" She stopped again and frowned, "then my grandmother committed suicide."

"Shit. That's horrible."

"Yeah, it gets worse. She drowned herself, threw herself into a lake. My grandfather saw her do it. He tried to save her and – in the end they both died. He couldn't swim, he was asthmatic, he'd never learnt but he jumped in anyway and they were both swept away."

All the stories, the rumours, flooded his brain. "Libby – not that lake?" he pointed across the grass. "It wasn't that lake was it?" She nodded. "Bloody hell."

"Yeah. So, afterwards my mum went to pieces, she completely lost it. She was put in a hospital. They kept them apart, her and my dad until after I was born. As soon as he got the chance, he took us away. He reckoned that being here was the cause of her problems, so he just collected us both one night and left. They got married; well back then I think you had to really."

"We moved around all the time," Libby continued. "He wouldn't let her talk about it and he wouldn't ever hear of coming back. He was right; she was never quite – erm – normal. She used to have terrible down times and over and over she had to go into hospital. There was often talk of her being committed but Dad managed to get her out each time. It was so hard for us all. Dad kept it together but then he was killed, a car accident." Her voice wavered and she had to raise a hand to brush away tears. "Now, things are different, care in the community they call it, but basically it means you're pretty much on your own most of the time. I tried to look after her, but it was all too hard and then one day I just couldn't do it anymore. I ran. I know I'm weak and horrible, but I just couldn't cope with it."

"But the house, Libby, how come you're here? How can you bear to be here?"

"I was in London and I was looking at the adverts for work, just cleaning and gardening and stuff, it's all I can do. We were never in one place long enough for me to get much in the way of exams. We were abroad some of the time, in Scotland for a while, way out in the wilds. Anyway, I saw the picture of the place; I couldn't believe it and I thought it would be cool. Sort of getting my own back, you know, getting to live here."

"My mum always said that it should have been ours, but we'd been cheated out of it. She had some pictures and she used to take them out when Dad wasn't there and cry over them. She said that they'd cut us off. She didn't seem to understand that Dad had done everything he could to make sure they couldn't contact us. We had PO Boxes for the mail, and he used to change the spelling of our name, little things like that. We kept moving, he was a carpenter and took cash in hand work on building sites or casual stuff. He was very bitter, he reckoned that if they'd just let them get married right at the start none of it would have happened, but I don't know. He was just trying to protect her, to protect both of us. Once I got older, I could see what was going on. She was eaten up with resentment and everything was twisted in her mind," she continued.

"Who is it that owns the house?"

"It's my aunt, or actually my great aunt. That's who I have been communicating with by email. I don't know where she is or anything though. You can't tell can you, not these days? She has no idea who I am."

"But everyone I've spoken to says that she's old and sick. The solicitor, the woman from the care agency."

"What care agency?"

"She had carers and then they were cancelled and they were told that her niece was moving in. That was you then, was it?"

"No, no that doesn't make sense. I never said I was related and anyway I've never seen her, I've never seen anyone. I haven't spoken to any care agencies. I've been on my own. No, I think you've got that wrong."

"But your mum, Libby, okay she has problems, but, well, she's still your mother." Before he had finished speaking Libby raised a hand to stop him and she shook her head.

"No, you don't have any idea. I bet you get on really well with your mum, don't you?"

"Yeah 'course. She's lovely my mum, fusses a bit now and then, but yeah we get on okay."

"So, you can't have any idea. She's so possessive. She's so – oh I don't know what the word is – needy I suppose. She just wanted me there all the time; she panicked if I was gone for more than an hour or so. She has screaming sessions and times when she just can't talk to anyone. She doesn't trust anyone, not even me. She used to go through my stuff. She once threw out all my clothes so I couldn't leave the house, she stuffed them in the Sally Army recycle bin. All I had was what I stood up in. She's not always so bad but you just never know what'll set her off or how long it's going to last. I know it looks bad that I left her; I know I should have stayed. But I had no life and she's not old – people used to sometimes think we were sisters. I couldn't face it, years and years of it."

"No, and you shouldn't have to. There must be help that you can get though, agencies and so on. Did you not ask for help?" She didn't answer him, just stared across the table, the frustration in her eyes. "But you could you know."

"Could what, Jed?" He saw the spark burn for a moment. "I could go backwards, back to where I had to run from. Really, I know it's selfish but I don't want to, I just don't want to. I wish she was okay. I wish she was happy but I couldn't do that for her, and there was this," she pushed up her sleeve to reveal an area of shiny puckered skin, "look, nice isn't it?"

"What's that, what happened to your arm?"

"A pan of soup."

"Oh God. Did she do that?" She didn't need to answer. She gently touched the damaged flesh.

"I've moved around all over the place, I even went to Spain, worked in a bar for a bit. I just needed to keep moving, I didn't want her to find me."

"There's the other thing isn't there?"

"What other thing?"

"Your great aunt, where is she? Didn't you say she was in Africa?"

"Did I? Oh right, right yes. Okay so I don't know, it's just that she used to live there, years and years ago, and so I just assumed, I guess. If she's sick though perhaps she's in a nursing home or something. I never met her; it was an agency that did the recruiting, you know, a temping agency. All they told me was that the main house was empty and I would have a flat."

"So how come you knew it was for sale – back at the bus stop when you first told me that it was to be sold?"

"It was a part of the contract that I would be expected to help when it was time for it to be sold. That's why it's a short-term contract, month to month. I told them I had a contact in the estate agency business – well I did once I found out where you caught the bus." She grinned at him and took a long drink. "I asked them to pass the message on to the owners. They did that and then she got in touch. Although, maybe it's not her, somebody working for her I suppose, if she's really old. I reckoned they might give me some commission or something."

"Fair enough, nothing wrong with that, enterprising of you really. So, it was just a coincidence?"

"Well, sort of, and a bit of sneaking about on my part to be honest, sorry about that. I guess I did sort of use you. I hung about in town, round your office, and I saw that you came home this way. I thought it'd be better than one of those stuffy old blokes. Then when you said your job was on the line, well it all fell into place. But yeah, I guess I used you. Sorry."

"Don't worry. It worked out for me didn't it, eh? It's a shame though, about you and your mum."

"Yeah, well it's just the way it is."

"You know this could be a good thing."

"What could?"

"Well why not let your aunt know who you are. Maybe she could help, maybe you could get your family back together."

Libby pursed her lips and shook her head. "I can't, I just can't. It's been a hell of a couple of years, really difficult, I've been skint most of the time, and sometimes I had to sleep rough. I've been used to struggling but this took it to a whole new level. You've no idea. And if I see her, if I go back it's all been for nothing. I can't."

"So, what will you do? After this I mean, where will you go?"

"Well, thing is, I knew this was all coming to an end. I'm not bothered, I've done what I wanted."

"What's that?"

"I've seen the place – lived in it, sort of and, you know –" She raised her hand and pointed towards the lake and the river in the distance. "Something like that, in your past – you wonder about it. Now I don't have to wonder anymore. I've seen where it happened; they went into that big pipe. They picked the bodies up in the river. My dad told me about it, trying to explain how horrible it was for her, why she was the way she was. Seeing it all I think helps me to understand her a bit better. I can see how she felt, that she had lost so much and became bitter. I don't feel the same; she used to tell me I'd been cheated but that doesn't feel right. Anyway, it's helped me to settle it in my mind a bit. I don't really know how much she actually saw. She never could talk about it without going to pieces. In the end the blame got shifted I think, especially after Dad died, she looked at me and saw me as the cause of all her troubles." She turned to watch the glow of red as it spread across the surface of the lake.

He would never tell her that he had seen her beside the water, sobbing. The things he had since discovered about her, made the guilt he already felt about his actions that day, even sharper.

"But, will you just move on, never see her again?"

"Yeah, just keep on going. I know you probably think I'm horrible but I need to live my life. I deserve that, don't I?"

She turned to look at him. Of course, she had a right to live as she wanted, but he didn't want her to go. There it was, the truth.

"How did you manage it, getting this job without letting them know who you are?"

"It wasn't hard. I learned from my dad that you only need to change things a bit to fog things up. My name, my full name is Elizabeth so Libby wouldn't click with anyone and Carlton is my middle name. When you're dealing with temping and casual agencies, they don't look into things too much, a couple of bills with your name on and it's pretty much enough for them."

"Trouble is now with the internet and everything you just don't know where your details are."

"No, but I don't see how she could find me, not really."

She slid a hand into her pocket and took out the thin cigarette, "D'ya want some?"

"No, no thanks. I don't like to do it often."

"Right. You probably think I'm at it all the time."

"None of my business really, is it?"

She gave a short laugh. "No but I see your face. Anyway, I don't use it so much." As she spoke, she peered down at her hand and, with a grin she just pushed the joint back into her pocket. "There you go, see I'm not an addict."

"No, I didn't think you were – well, I didn't think about it really that much." As he lied, he felt his face growing warm.

"You are funny, Jed. You know sometimes you seem so – oh what's the word – innocent."

"You think I'm a wuss."

"No, it's nice. You've had an easier life than me, haven't you? It shows."

He took a chance, "Have you used other stuff?"

"No, I haven't. Never been tempted to be honest, not after I've watched my mum. Why?"

"It's just that one time you said you could tell me about other stuff, stronger, scarier."

"Yeah, I could. My mum, believe it or not, is pretty clever, well she was at one time. She has a degree in pharmacology. She always said she was going back to work, but it was all a load of rot. She couldn't hold down a job, not now. She had the books though, and the magazines and she used to keep an eye on things on the internet."

"So, she doesn't work?"

"Nah, but Dad left her taken care of thank God – insurance, and he made sure it was all tied up so she couldn't just spend it all. He knew she wouldn't cope with finances. She's not desperately short of money but a fair bit of it goes on the stuff she uses. Some of it was on prescription and some of it not. I learned a lot by keeping an eye on her medication."

"He sounds pretty special, your dad."

"Yeah, but they never gave him a chance, her family. Anyway, come on let's go and eat and talk about something else, that's all rather depressing. You can tell me what you think they're going to do with this place. I bet it's going to be nice. There's loads of potential, isn't there?"

"Yeah, there is." And they turned and climbed the few stairs back to her small home.

* * *

I am going to die soon now, I drift, I don't feel the cold so much anymore. I have seen my mother. She was smiling at me, Estelle was there also, she was crying. Don't cry lovely Estelle, we'll be together soon and all the problems, all the fear and the worry, all the despair, will be over. I am ready.

My mind is clear. Clearer than it has been in an age. I know I am dehydrated and breathing is agony. I have no strength; I can no longer reach the bucket to pass water. I have not needed it for a long time now, and so in a way the dehydration is a blessing, though I know it will contribute to my demise. Every movement sends shards of agony through my body but my mind is clear while I am awake. When I sleep, and mostly I am in a stupor, I dream, I hallucinate that I am diving into deep pools, swimming in crystal water and then I see it so clearly. Estelle and Francis, and the horror of it all, and always the same outcome and nothing ever to be done, I can't bear it.

So, at the end I can think and remember and grieve, but I can do nothing because I simply don't have the strength and anyway it's all too late.

Why, why has she done this? For many years I have searched and searched for her, to ask her to forgive us, all of us, for our narrow-minded attitude and our snobbish behaviour.

All too late and nothing to do now but wait for the end and pray that it is soon.

145

Chapter 38

"This is lovely, Libby." Jed wiped round his plate with a piece of baguette.

"I used to make stuff a fair bit, when I was with her."

"It's sad, really unfair and sad."

"Yeah well, I've learned that the only thing you can do is just get on with it. It was okay when my dad was around, he was so good with her. After he'd gone though, she just got worse and worse. I should go back, shouldn't I?" She had lowered her head and was fiddling with the edge of the breakfast bar, running her nail back and forth along the rim. "I know I should look after her. She's my mum after all and she's got nobody else."

"But she must be able to function, if you could leave her."

"Oh yes, she can. A lot of the time you wouldn't know there was anything wrong with her, but when she freaks out, she's hopeless, and she can't look after herself. Over the last couple of years, every now and again I have nearly gone back. I've thought about her, maybe sitting on her own, her clothes dirty, not eating and I've felt so guilty. But I know if I go back that's it for me – for ever."

"How old is she, Libby?"

"She's in her early forties. You wouldn't think it to look at her though; she's slim, same build as me really. When she's not well she doesn't eat and the weight drops off her but yeah, really she's about the same as me. We used to get mistaken for sisters sometimes." He thought about the desk set and the woman he'd seen in the street near the office.

"Do you think she might have been here before?"

"Hmm, no, I don't think so, how could she? Why?" He must tread carefully now.

"It's just that you did say that sometimes the place seemed disturbed."

"Yeah, that's right. But, no, I mean why would she?"

"Do you think that maybe she has just come back? Come home?"

"I guess that's possible, it's not likely though – is it? She can't be living here, can she? I mean if there was someone living here, I'd know." As she looked at him, he could see something like doubt creep into her eyes.

"What?"

"Okay, the thing is that the temping agency told me that the house was empty. All I'm supposed to do is go in now and again and do a walk around. I have to make sure there are no water leaks or anything, that sort of thing. I have to keep the garden a bit under control but just stuff like picking up the apples in case of rats and making sure nobody comes in and wrecks it all."

"Yes."

"Oh, this is going to sound stupid."

"Go on."

"Just sometimes I've been in there and I'd have this feeling, just a sort of idea that there was somebody there. I don't believe in ghosts, at least I don't think I do, but now and again I sort of wondered if the place was haunted." She turned away, her face had reddened. "Oh, listen to me – haunted, it's ridiculous, stupid. Don't take any notice."

"Maybe she has been coming without you knowing?"

"But, why would she do that, why not just live in it or something?"

"I don't know," he said slowly, carefully, "perhaps if she's so bitter, maybe she thought she could take some things. You know, if she feels as though she's entitled to something from the family." He stopped as she shook her head again.

"But, how would she know it was empty, Jed? How would she know that my great aunt isn't here? Nobody else knows where Mrs Carmody is, how could she? Anyway, there's nothing missing, I'd have noticed."

"Are you sure?"

"Well, unless it was really small stuff yeah, I mean if there was furniture or whatever, I'd notice. I go in a couple of times a week."

He wouldn't push it any more now, he felt relieved, but there was something more important on his mind. "What are you going to do, Libby? You can't just take off and leave."

"I can, I've done it before. It's easier than you'd think."

"But, have you thought about this? If this house belongs to your great aunt maybe you should try and let her know who you are. Just tell her the truth and maybe you don't have to be on your own."

"No, no – I've got no family. No, that's not the way it's going to be. I'm on my own, I just am. Remember, Jed, they didn't want me; we weren't good enough, me and my dad. No, I don't want anything from this family. Shit, I got my mum and that's more than enough. Oh, sorry I shouldn't have said that, this wine, it's gone to my head a bit."

* * *

I am still here, why? Please take me now. If there is a God, if there are angels, carry me away. I can't abide any more. Why am I still here when people die suddenly the world over? Have I been so evil that I must suffer so greatly, for so long? Take me now.

Chapter 39

"I'll tell you what though, Jed. I'll stay as long as I can. I'll stay until the paperwork is all done and I have to go. How long do you reckon that will be?"

"It could be a while yet, a couple of weeks at the very least. There's no problem with funding, the solicitors will do searches, but most of that has already been done by the developer's legal team anyway, so fingers crossed it'll all be smooth and easy. The contract was in the last package for your aunt to sign. Sometimes there can be hiccups just before completion, but I hope not, that's why we were so careful about who we took this to."

"That sounds odd, you saying that. I'd never really thought about the fact that I was dealing with a relative."

"If you like we can carry on calling her 'the owner'."

"Yes, I'd rather. Anyway, that stuff should come back in the next day or so."

"That's great, Libby, I like the idea of you sticking around for a bit." She grinned at him, the quirky, cheeky grin that he had come to like so much.

"There is something else though," she said.

"What's that?"

"Do you remember you tried to give me a phone a while back?"

"Yes, I've got it here, in my work bag."

"If it's still on offer I wouldn't mind having it now. I was being a bit high maintenance and stupid and actually I wouldn't mind having one. If you give me that, I can ring you when the paperwork comes back. It'll make things easier."

He rooted in his bag and brought out the shiny box. "It's not an expensive one you know. Just a phone, no internet or anything."

"It's okay, I don't do much of that stuff, just now and again if I need to search for something, or check my mail, more just now with all this going on, but – well." She swept her hand around her, taking in the little flat and the laptop on the work top in the kitchen. "This is me, small and ordinary."

"It's nice though, Libby, really cosy." She turned her head to look at the compact space.

"Yeah it's been a nice place to live."

"It's a shame you didn't know about it before, you might have been able to come and stay; it's your family after all."

"No, you're not listening to me. This is not my family; this is nothing to do with who I am except for history. Anyway, it's all being sold now."

"Yes. That's true. Right, as I said my contact details are in there and I have the number of that phone in my own. If you need me, Libby – if ever you need me, just ring."

She laughed. "I've never had a bodyguard before."

"Don't be daft – I just meant, you know, if you wanted someone to talk to, to have a drink with."

"What you mean like a friend?"

"Yeah."

"Hmm, I never had one of those before either."

"It's time for me to go. This has been nice, Libby. I'm sorry about all your trouble but yeah, this has been a nice evening."

"Okay, you can go down the main drive, I need to lock the gates in a bit. I opened them for the bloke who does the grass."

"Do you want a hand, with the dishes and stuff?"

"No, no I'm a bit of a fusser, it's better if I do it myself."

She went with him to the door and this time he bent and gave her a quick kiss on the cheek. She pulled back and raised her hand to her face and he was surprised to see her blush. Before she could become more embarrassed, he turned and jogged down the steps. He strode out down the grand drive towards the main gates. He knew that she was standing at the top of the steps watching as he disappeared into the gloom.

Just a few minutes later, in the vegetable garden a rat nibbling at an overlooked windfall lifted its head, turned and scurried away from the slender shadow moving towards the back of the house.

* * *

She had no fear of the dark, Libby had known for a long time that sometimes dreadful things happen in the full glare of the sun. She took a torch in case but didn't bother to turn it on. The night was cool with a waning moon silvering the partly denuded branches. She stopped for a moment to listen to the shift and sway, and the faint sound of the river in the distance.

* * *

"Sarah, is it you?"

"Of course, it's me, you stupid woman. You have to understand that now there is only me, no nurses, no home help, just me."

151

"What do you want, Sarah? Just tell me and I'll give you anything if you will only take me back to my room."

"Oh no, you can let that idea go – you have no room, you have no home, you have nothing, just this bottle of water, here you are, that's what you have left."

"Oh, thank you, thank you. Put it into my hand please, I can't see."

"Yes, you can have it but first sign this…"

"More papers, what are they all? Oh, it doesn't matter, help me, I can't hold the pen, guide my hand, help me and then give me the drink. But, Sarah – please don't lock me in again, don't leave me I beg you, please just take me back to my room. I'll give you anything, anything."

"You have nothing, nothing to give me. Here, take your water."

Chapter 40

"Mail for you, Jed."

"Thanks, Molly, bit early isn't it?"

"Came by courier."

"Ah, okay. Oh."

"What, something wrong?"

"No, well not really. It's the stuff for The Willows."

"Brilliant. That's really great."

"Yeah, it is. Did you say it came by courier?"

"Yes, a motorbike bloke. Is there something wrong with it? I'd have thought you'd be dancing on the desk."

"No, it's just that I expected… Have there been any phone calls for me, Molly?"

"No, not 'specially." He pulled his phone from his pocket but there were no texts, no missed calls. He had thought that they had crossed over into a real friendship and was hurt and disappointed that Libby had sent the papers without contacting him first. He replayed the evening in his mind; they had parted on good terms, hadn't they? He expected she would be at the bus stop, but sat alone waiting for the number three and assumed she had other things to do. It didn't matter as much now he had a means of communicating with her, but this – did this mean

that she didn't want to use the phone after all? And if so –
why? And what should he do? She was such a complicated
woman; okay he could understand some of it, but it was
bloody hard work trying to get to know her.

He picked up the sheaf of documents and carried them
upstairs to Charles's office. They would need to be
examined closely and then that was it. Just the nits to pick
at, and there shouldn't be many of those and it was over.
He would have his lump of commission in the bank and
the boost to his standing. Everything he had been hoping
for.

"Phone for you, Jed, a woman." Aha, it was all okay
after all; this would be Libby to tell him the stuff was on its
way.

"Hi, there. I've got them already."

"I'm sorry, is that Mr Carlisle?"

"Oh, yes – who is this?"

"I have Mr Michael Irwin for you, please hold."

"Right, sorry."

"Hello, Jed, Mike here."

"Morning, Mr Irwin, what can I do for you?"

"I'm calling about The Willows."

"Yes, I have the contract here, Mr Irwin – it came in a
few minutes ago."

"Hmm. I have received some communication myself. I
am concerned, I'm afraid this is all rather odd and is
making me very uncomfortable about the whole thing, Jed.
As you know, I have had some reservations, and this
document this morning is rather unsettling."

Shit. "What is it that you've had? Is it a planning
problem?"

"No, nothing like that. It's a letter purporting to come
from Mrs Carmody. We have held her will for some
considerable time and this is rather at odds with our
current instructions. The document is signed but there are
no witness signatures, which would make it dubious in any
event."

"Oh, well I suppose under the circumstances that's not a surprise, with the change in her situation and all."

"Yes, as you say, but the change in the bequest is startling, and I am not happy – not happy at all."

"Oh." *Come on get on with it, you old windbag, what's going on?*

"I am speaking in confidence, Jed, and it's only because I am so very concerned and she is after all a mutual client. You see the estate was always to be left to the niece, Sarah, and if she was deceased to the niece's daughter, Elizabeth. The total estate after the usual fees and payment of debts in the normal way, all very simple really."

Jed was speechless. Elizabeth, Libby – she was going to inherit the proceeds of the sale, millions. Maybe not now but eventually and she had no idea. She would be rich, all she had to do was get in touch with her aunt and say who she was.

"Of course, they have to be found. The family searched for a long time with no success, but money was set aside for a further investigation and I have no doubt that, with widespread advertising and the improvement in communications, there would be a much better chance of making contact, especially if there were a bequest involved – human nature being what it is. I was going to suggest a renewed attempt with our client anyway, in view of the major changes to her situation. Mainly because The Willows would no longer be her address. Anyway, that was before this, erm, bombshell this morning."

He should speak, he should tell this crusty old bloke that he knew exactly where they were, but could he? Could he betray Libby's confidence? He held his tongue.

"You see, this new letter, it instructs us to direct payment from the sale of the estate directly into an account for Sarah, there are account details and what have you. It's very odd and we can't, you do see don't you, we just can't."

"What?" He knew he had raised his voice, he coughed, muttered an apology.

"Exactly, as I say, a bit of a bombshell. "I'm sorry, Jed, but I am going to have to insist that everything is put on hold for the moment. I can't in all conscience accept this. I feel that we are duty bound to investigate and to confirm to our total satisfaction that this is in fact a true reflection of Mrs Carmody's wishes, that the details are all correct. We have to assume now that she is in touch with her niece but I must have confirmation of all of that. I am going to have to insist on speaking to her directly. It may take some time, after all we are not really sure where she is at the moment. The envelope was hand delivered apparently, a courier; there is no franking or stamp. I realise this could complicate things at your end, but it can't be helped. I have to say this development sheds doubt yet again on the whole situation. We need to have a meeting, all of us, with the partners over there. I'll have my assistant get onto that right away. I am sorry, Jed, but I'm sure you understand. Good day."

"Right, yes, oh erm, goodbye Mr Irwin. Yes, thanks."

He took out his phone and keyed in the fast dial for the phone he had given Libby. It rang long enough for the auto cut-off to activate and leave him staring blankly at the little grey handset in his palm.

Chapter 41

First Libby was aware of pain, then there was the cold and there was the dark. She was confused, disoriented, and before she had the chance to move, her stomach revolted and vomit spewed in a small pool on the grubby flags. "Oh god – shit. What the hell has happened?"

"Hello, Sarah, is that you Sarah? Did you fall?" A voice whispered in the darkness.

"Oh, bloody hell."

"Are you sick? Have you been sick? Oh Sarah, where are you? I can't help you." The feeble cry was pathetic and panicked.

"I'm okay, I'm okay. Where is this though, where the hell am I?"

"Sarah?"

"No, no – I'm not Sarah. Who are you? Where are you? Hang on, my eyes are getting used to the dark, just give me a sec. I'm dizzy. What is going on? Oh hell."

"What, what's the matter?"

"My head is throbbing. I've got a bloody great lump on it."

"Did you fall?"

"Yes, I guess so, I must'a' done. I don't remember."

"Are you hurt?"

"I've hurt my hand I think; I've bashed my knee. It's okay though, I don't think anything's broke. I feel nauseous, just give me a minute."

"Who are you?"

"Hang on. I'm going to try and come over to you. I think I can see you. Can you move your arms or something? Okay, I see you. I'm coming over." Libby scrambled across the gritty floor and dragged herself upwards. Bracing a hand against the damp wall she leaned towards the dark shape stretched on a platform a couple of feet from the ground. She reached out and touched the pale hand lying against a darker bulk.

"Oh, oh thank you. Who are you? Hold my hand, please don't let go."

"Okay, okay, but keep calm, ow, that hand is sore. Here, let me sit down."

"Who are you? How is it that you're here?"

"Libby, my name's Libby. I'm the caretaker at The Willows. Do you know where this is? What is this place?"

"It's The Willows, dear. It's the cellar. Thank God, thank God I've been found."

"But, how the hell did you get in here? Who are you? Why are you down here if it's the cellar?"

"I don't know, I just don't know. I've been ill, very ill, and I was in my room asleep. I had some trouble with my carers and then Sarah came. My niece, she was helping me and then…"

"Oh, don't cry, please don't cry. You're cold, aren't you? This bed is damp. Here, let me wrap my coat around you."

"You are good, so kind. Thank you, thank you so much. Who are you, dear?"

"Libby, I said. Libby, I'm the caretaker."

"But I don't have a caretaker. We have never had a caretaker. We had a gardener and some help in the house. I had home nursing and carers but something happened, they stopped them coming, I think someone did, I get confused. No, you must be mistaken, we never had a caretaker."

"I am, honestly. I live above the garage."

"No, no you don't. I don't understand."

"Oh, well it doesn't matter for now does it? God, my head is pounding. Are there no lights here?"

"No, no power at all. Nothing, it's just a storage cellar. We used oil lamps in the old days, but nobody has been down here for an age."

"What are you lying on? I have looked in here before, there was no furniture. Are you sure it's the cellar?"

"Yes, I think this is one of the shelves. There's a sort of thin mattress but it's damp, it's all damp and I'm so cold. Can't you get us out, dear? Can't you try and get us out, just take me back…"

"Hey, hey – are you okay? Hello?"

"What, oh, oh – you mustn't worry. I can't stay awake for very long. I drift away. It's alright. I've been ill, did I say I've been ill. I don't know you though, I don't recognise you."

"I'm Libby, don't you remember? I'm Libby."

"Oh, yes Libby. Sorry. I can't talk anymore."

"It's okay. You just rest. I did have a torch."

"Why are you here?"

"I was closing the gates. I heard a noise and I just walked through the garden to see. I don't really remember what happened. I must have slipped, or…"

"Or what, dear?"

"No, nothing, it's nothing. Don't worry. I'm going back over to the steps now to see if I can find my torch."

"Don't leave me, please don't leave me."

"Don't panic. I won't leave you. I promise I won't leave you. Please don't cry."

"Keep talking to me, keep talking. I can't see you very well and if you move into the dark, I can't see you at all. Just talk to me."

"Yes, I will. Don't worry I won't leave you. I'll sort all this out. Just let me see if I can find my torch. Oh… shit."

"What, what is it? What's wrong, have you hurt yourself?"

"No, it's just that the torch is in bits. I don't think I can fix this. Oh well. I can see a bit now. We'll have to manage."

"Is the door locked?"

"Hold on. Yes, yes it's locked solid. But how can that be? If I tripped – oh…"

"It's Sarah, isn't it? She's locked us in. I was so happy when she came back but I don't know why she's done this. Do you know Sarah? Do you know why she has done this?"

"Bloody hell, the heartless bitch. Okay, let's just keep calm okay? Let's just keep calm and see if we can work out what to do eh?"

"Yes, but just don't leave me on my own again."

"No, I won't. I won't leave you."

Chapter 42

"Hello, are you awake? Are you okay?"

"I'm awake, dear. Yes, I'm awake but I'm not well, not well at all."

"No, I know you're not, but try and hang on. Keep talking to me. Let me get on there, beside you." Libby slid partway onto the damp ledge and wrapped her arms around the frail shivering body. "There, that's better isn't it?"

"Oh yes, that's much better. Thank you, thank you so much. You are very kind. Did you say you have been living in the garage apartment?"

"Yeah, that's it."

"Well, it's odd. I didn't know anything about it. I wonder if it was the care agency. But, why would they do that without telling me? Oh dear, I have been very silly, haven't I?"

"No, I don't think you have, what would you want to say that for?"

"I let things get out of control, my father always insisted that you must keep control, you must run your own life. It all became too hard though."

She must keep the old woman talking, talking might stop her worrying, but she drifted away often and Libby had to shake her gently to bring her back.

"Why did it get hard? Didn't you have anyone to help?"

"No, dear – I have been on my own for a long time now. I used to have a family, a lovely family but it all went wrong; we fragmented and were split asunder. Ripped apart by pride and shame, and by insanity. I lost my husband, and then I fell and after that it all becomes a blur. I was dizzy so much lately and sick and the nice carers stopped coming…"

"Shh shh, don't cry." Libby was rocking back and forth, cradling the old woman, her great aunt, in the dark.

She wanted to move and to act, but couldn't cruelly withdraw her body heat from the other. She had no idea how long they sat, but her legs became numb, and cold seeped into her bones and then creeping despair robbed her of the ability to make conversation. Marian was muttering, quiet, unintelligible, broken words, winding and drifting from some inner world and at last Libby felt the weight on her arms increase and knew that her aunt slept. How strange it was after all these years of listening to her mother's outpourings of bitterness and blame to find herself rocking this poor old thing and warming her with her own body heat. She stroked the wrinkled cheek. She had to get her out, and back to a proper warm bed. She needed to get some fluids into her.

Her childhood had been spent as part of a tight little group of three, hiding and moving on and sometimes wondering what it was like to have a granny to visit or a cousin to play with. She had seen other children hugged and taken up in caresses and she had felt the loss of what had never been hers and built a carapace against it, and now it had cracked in this dismal space, and regret had sneaked in. She whispered into the darkness, "I'm sorry, Marian. I really am." And as she spoke, a tear of her own joined those the old woman had shed.

She had to do something, to try to find a way out but as she shifted her legs, Marian stirred. The bulk of her rolled and she groaned. "Sshh, shh, it's okay. You're okay I've got you."

"Where am I, where is this?"

"We're in the cellar, don't you remember?"

"Oh, Estelle – is that you Estelle? Mother will be angry. We're not supposed to come down here."

"No, no it's me, it's Libby."

"Libby, I don't know anyone called Libby. Let me go, let me up. I don't know you." She began to struggle, pushing against the arms around her and flailing out at Libby who was on the edge of the shelf, one leg over the side with her foot on the floor to steady herself. "Let me go, let me down, what have you done? Where's Estelle? What have you done to Estelle?"

"It's alright, really. I haven't hurt Estelle. She died. Don't you remember Estelle died? She drowned in the lake."

"Estelle, oh Estelle." Marian pushed upwards, her fingers clawed at the dirty bricks and she strained sideways against the wall. "Help me someone – please get me out, please." Libby recognised that the last vestige of reality had been stolen by the uneasy sleep, but she was desperate to find a way to reach the worn out and confused mind.

"Don't be afraid, don't cry. Aunty Marian, don't be afraid. It's me, it's Elizabeth. I'm not going to hurt you now."

There was a minute of silence as Marian sagged back and calmed and then a feeble whisper threaded into the gloom. "Elizabeth, no there is no Elizabeth, there was a baby, many years ago but she's gone, they've all gone. No, there is no Elizabeth."

"There is, I'm here, I came back. I came to see you." The bending of the truth was of no moment if it gave some comfort. Her confusion was so great it hardly mattered what was said as long as it helped to calm the old woman's fears. "I came to meet you, Aunty Marian. To spend some time with you."

"Elizabeth, Sarah's daughter? Is it true, is she here also? Is Sarah with you?" There seemed little point trying to make her remember recent happenings or to rehash the betrayals and the lies. There was just this moment. What had brought them to it was unimportant.

"She's waiting to see you. When we get out of here, we're all going to spend some time together. We can catch up; we can get to know each other."

"Oh, how wonderful, I have longed for this for so many years. And is it true, are you really Elizabeth? I wish I could see you; if there was some light, I could see you." She sighed.

"Yes, Aunty Marian, I wish you could see me as well."

But as Libby felt the old body sag and grow heavy in her arms, she understood that their eyes would never meet and that these moments in a dingy cellar would be the only ones she would spend with her extended family.

"Bloody hell. No. I'm so sorry, Aunty Marian, but I didn't know, I didn't know you were down here," and she rocked the wasted frame and was overcome with guilt.

She didn't cry but slid out from under the still body and then straightened the limbs, pulled the blanket over her and tucked it under the old lady's chin, and then she turned away and walked back to the dark flight of steps. She had to find a way out, and then it was all going to have to be faced because Marian had died as a direct result of being locked in this place. Did this then mean that her mother had crossed the final line and had become a murderer? The thought brought a flush of nausea and she pushed it aside. First, she must get free. Then they would have to find a way to deal with the rest of it.

Chapter 43

The meeting was tense. Jed had tried repeatedly to call Libby and decided that she must have left the phone in its box. Probably she hadn't seen the need to carry it with her now that the papers had come through. He had the contract and so she might never use it. He was in the conference room with Charles and Mike Irwin, trying to explain the details of his communication with the owners of the estate without letting them all realise just how fragile the whole thing had been.

"Who exactly is your contact at The Willows?" Charles had wanted to know.

"It's a person retained by the family. Mr Irwin has met her; I believe you were quite impressed weren't you, Mike?"

"So, you have never spoken directly to the owner?"

"Well, not as such no, but I am in almost daily contact with the representative."

"Where exactly is their office?"

"Ah, no. They, well she – it's a young woman, she doesn't have an office. It's a bit casual I know, but seems to have worked up to now."

Mr Irwin was frowning and constantly fiddling with the file he had brought with him.

"We need her phone number. My office is going to have to be in touch," he said. Jed nodded and shifted in his seat.

"Yes, well I believe she has only recently got her phone number activated. I will contact her as soon as I can and ask her to call you, or maybe pop into your office."

"Well, Jed, if you simply give us her number, then we can probably set up some lines of communication this afternoon."

"Uhu, I feel a little awkward giving out her contact details without letting her know first." He glanced at Charles who was beginning to glower at him.

"I am sure Mr Irwin can be trusted with telephone numbers, Jed."

Jed managed a sort of embarrassed laugh, but by now everyone was becoming short-tempered and irritated. He was looking more and more ridiculous.

"I'll contact her immediately. I have tried already today but had no response. It may be best if I simply call round and see her."

"Fine, I'll come with you. After all, the only thing I need from this person is a means of approaching Mrs Carmody directly in order to set up a meeting, yes? I suppose we need to go out there, to The Willows."

"Why don't I go now. I expect I'll find her at the property."

"Fine, come along let's get going."

"Oh, erm I don't know for certain that's where she'll be of course." Charles sighed and began tapping his finger nails on the polished top of the conference table.

He was going to have to take them, wasn't he? Libby would be furious, but there was no other way around it. He had begun to hope that perhaps they could remain friends or even something more. Now though there was this. Also, he had no idea how she might react to the news about her possible inheritance. Being Libby, he didn't imagine for one moment that she would simply break out the champagne and book a cruise.

The others were pulling together their papers; Mike Irwin was sliding files back into his battered brown briefcase. It didn't look as though there was any way to avoid a whole parade of them turning up at Libby's front door.

Irwin's phone danced across the table. He picked it up and peered at the screen. "Oh, sorry. Please excuse me gentlemen I do need to take this." Charles nodded his approval and Jed simply stared out of the window. He felt miserable and embarrassed. It was like being in the headmaster's study, knowing he was about to get into hot water.

He hadn't done anything actually wrong, neither had Libby, but it was just not quite right either. He needed to speak to her on his own first, to prepare her and maybe even help her to avoid meeting these people at all if that was what she wanted. She was possibly going to be forced to admit just who she was and how she had become involved in all of this and he knew it might make her run. He was convinced that if she disappeared now, he would never see her again. He was aware of the solicitor mumbling into his handset and then slipping the phone into his pocket.

"Oh well, it seems that I am going to have to get back to the office right away. This is most annoying but there is no way around it. Look, Jed, you really must organise some way for me to either meet with Miss Carlton or at the very least speak to her by telephone. As far as we are concerned nothing can progress now until we have spoken directly to Mrs Carmody and it seems that this is the most direct route, and even this seems to be unduly complicated."

He snatched up his things and with a nod to the room in general he stomped out into the hallway.

Before Charles had a chance to speak, Jed jumped to his feet. "Right, I'm on it. I'm going to go up to The Willows right now and sort this out." The speed and decisiveness took the wind out of the other man's sails.

"Fine, off you go, but Jed..."

"Yes."

"Get this sorted, get this sorted today. You have to put Mike in touch with Mrs Carmody pretty damn quickly. I haven't told them over at Langleys, but they are going to want to know what the hold-up is if I don't get back to them in a day or two with an update."

"Don't worry Charles, I'm going to fix it." He ran back down the narrow stairs and grabbed his coat. "I'm out, Molly, don't think I'll be back today but I'm on my phone."

Chapter 44

Moving about helped to keep her warm. Looking for a way out filled enough of Libby's mind to hold at bay the thought of what had happened with her great aunt who was just yards away across the cellar.

She pushed at the door, kicked it and then tried to worm her fingers into the tiny gap at the bottom, all of which got her nowhere. It was an old door, but made of solid timbers that flaked tiny crumbs of wood but it didn't give against the onslaught of her pounding feet and thumping fists.

She sat on the step, pulled the plastic lighter from her pocket and flipped the switch. The tiny flickering flame depressed her; it didn't light the space enough to be of any use, but it sent shadows dancing across the blanket-covered form. She closed the top and walked in the dimness back to the wall. Perhaps after all it was a mistake, maybe Marian wasn't dead. She wasn't a doctor, what did she know? Maybe the old woman was sleeping, just in a coma. She stretched out a hand and touched the pale face. The skin was cold and devoid of the spring of living flesh. She bent her head close, there wasn't the faintest stirring of air; there was no hint of life.

A feeling of complete aloneness was greater than the sadness, in truth she hadn't known this woman and her whole childhood had been spent running from her. She was sorry that the end had been hard and comfortless, but felt nothing like the devastating grief that had shocked her in its ferocity after her dad had been killed.

Should she cover the face? It's what people normally did, but really it didn't matter. It was dark and anyway she wasn't disturbed by it at all, it was more upsetting feeling so helpless. She thumped the wall in frustration. It was really scary to think her mother had done this because it indicated a further slip into the madness that plagued her. Did she know she had pushed her own daughter down into this horrible space? And if so, did she intend to come back, and when?

Apart from the steps there was nowhere else to sit and so she perched on the end of the shelf at the feet of her great aunt. "So, Aunty Marian, this is a mess isn't it?" She leaned back against the wall, her headache had eased but she was thirsty, cold and very weary. If Mum didn't come back it was two weeks until the gardener was due and there was no-one else expected, unless of course Jed came. She thought of the phone he had given her, it lay on the breakfast bar, she had been going to charge it and it had amused her that she would have her first phone, but it was of no use to her now. She had an idea that it wouldn't have worked here anyway, they didn't work in tunnels and such like as far as she knew. Her conscience was fighting with the idea that maybe she had to take part of the blame for Marian's death. Had she tried hard enough? Would it have been possible to have done anything else? It was hard to see how; the woman had been just hours from the end when Libby had found her, but what of the days before? She had been told that the cellar was locked and hadn't bothered to investigate and it was so very obvious now that she should have done.

She pushed her hand into her pocket, took out a spliff and lit up, "Hope you don't mind Marian but right now, I think I need this. And I'm sorry, I'm really bloody sorry, I know it doesn't make any soddin' difference but, well there we are." She drew in a great lungful of the smoke and closed her eyes.

* * *

Jed had tried the new mobile number repeatedly, but it was only something to do as he rode in the taxi through town and out towards The Willows. He paid the driver and pushed open the side gate. The front door at the top of the flight of concrete stairs was open. He jogged up the steps and knocked on the door frame. "Hello. Libby, it's me. It's Jed, I need a word."

After a few minutes he gave another shout "Hello. Libby, are you in there?" He could just push open the door and go inside; he would if this had been one of his other friends but not her, not Libby.

He turned on the landing and looked out across the grounds. It wasn't particularly cold so maybe she had just stepped out, perhaps to the vegetable garden, or to check the mail. He peered down the long drive. The main gates were closed, he would need to have a walk around, see if he could find her. He tried the phone again but knew already it just wasn't going to work.

He ran back down the steps and across the paved pathway to the kitchen entrance to find that it was locked. He peered through the window and all was in darkness.

With a sigh he turned back towards the garage. He'd go back to the bedsit. He'd have to speak to her, there was absolutely no way he could go back into the office without some sort of arrangement for a meeting.

"Libby, it's Jed. Can I come in? I need to have a chat." He pushed harder now against the door and it swung back giving him a better view of the inside.

The plates from their meal of the previous night were piled on the draining board which was clearly visible across the small lounge space. The coffee cups and glasses were still on the low table.

Alarm tickled at his nerve endings. She had told him she was going to tidy up, had said that she was a fuss pot, so why had she not done it? He could see the phone now on top of the box, with the instruction leaflet and charger beside it.

There was no sign of life and with a sick feeling in his stomach, he allowed the thought that had been niggling at the back of his mind to come forward. She had been upset, she used drugs, she said nothing more than the smokes but well... He knew now that he was going into her bedroom, and her bathroom, and he dreaded what he might find.

His heart pounded as he turned the plastic handle and opened the door. All he saw was a neatly made bed with a dressing gown laying across the bottom and he puffed out a sigh of relief. The door to the en-suite bathroom stood open and he could see immediately that it was empty. He blew out a gust of a sigh. Back outside he lowered himself to the top step. He would just have to wait for her. She could not have gone far, not having left the door open. He would wait.

Chapter 45

Where the hell was she? It was dusk and he was cold. Jed felt stupid sitting on the steps next to the open door, he should just go inside. She might be okay with that, but with Libby, who knew? He walked down the steps and beyond the flower borders, out onto the stretch of grass beside the main drive. As he scanned the area, a beam of low sunlight shot from between the clouds and painted a crimson line across the dark water, just visible across the long stretch of lawn.

Oh shit, the water, the bloody lake.

He began to run, his smooth soles slipping on the damp grass. Clouds swallowed up the brief glimpse of evening sun and the water grew black and menacing. His mind replayed the story of Estelle and her husband, pulled into the drainage pipe by the current. He was panicked and breathless when he reached the banks and clambered across the rocks and gravel. There was no sign of her. The drain was over at the far side, he couldn't reach it, not without plunging into the deep and dangerous water. He spun round and climbed back across the boulders into long grass and rushes.

He knew there was no point in running, he knew that, but he couldn't help it. He understood that if Libby was in the lake or swept into the river, she would have been all the time he had sat on the steps, maybe all the time since just after he had last seen her at the door the night before, then there was no point in running. He carried on running. He called her name. He knew there was no point to this either, but the yell left his throat of its own volition. "Libby, Libby!"

He couldn't see any sign of her. He had reached the far bank and clambered down the slippery, muddied slope to the soggy border of the water. Hands clutching at overhanging branches and sometimes on all fours, he struggled forward. His throat burned as the cold air scalded it and the struggle in the sucking, sticky mud caused him to wheeze and gasp.

He was at the entrance to the pipe. Water gushed into it singing and echoing as it rushed towards the far end where it cascaded back into the river. The current was obvious now, twigs and leaves swirled and tumbled in the flow, but now he saw fitted across the entrance was a great metal grill. Obviously set there after the tragedy, it ensured that nobody could be taken through, no-one would ever again be killed in the way that Libby's grandparents had been, and more importantly Libby was not here. She was not out in the river. The sudden withdrawal of adrenaline left him weakened and unable to do anything more than lean back against the bank and wait for his heart to slow and his shaking, shivering limbs to calm.

He opened his eyes and looked down at his clothes and hands, he was filthy, his trousers soaked and snagged in several places. Shaking his head at his over-reaction and the image he must have made galloping across the grounds shouting for the girl, he stood for a minute hands on his hips as he watched the endless gush of water. It was almost fully dark. He was wet and filthy and it was time to call it a day. He would come back in the morning. He didn't like it, not at all, he would have been much happier to find her safe and well. Not just because of the problems with the sale but also because of a genuine concern for her well-being.

As he strode back round the edge of the lake past the rocks where she had sat crying that day, he was struck by a terrible need to see her. He cared about her and hated to leave without making sure she was alright. He would go back to the flat, leave a note and ask her to call him when she came home.

In the low light he could easily have missed her but there she was, moving through the tiny wood. He yelled out. It seemed she hadn't seen him because she turned and walked further into the gloom between the trees.

"Libby, hey hang on. Libby – it's me, Jed."

But she carried on and in a very short time was swallowed up by the darkness. Now what should he do? He could go after her, into the trees, or go back to the flat and wait. Surely she wouldn't be staying out in the dark, not now it was getting really cold. Then again maybe it was just time to cut his losses and go home, have a hot shower and a huge glass of his dad's best malt and come back tomorrow, early. She was alright, he'd seen her – maybe she simply wanted to be left alone with the mounting problems, okay he could respect that. He'd leave a note and see her tomorrow.

* * *

Libby leaned over the body. "Hey, Marian, do you mind if I borrow your blanket?" She gently pulled the thin, damp covering towards her. "Thanks, I'll give it back later," she said and pulling it around her like a shroud she curled in the corner of the cellar, lowered her head onto her knees and tried not to shiver too much. In spite of the cold and the emotional overload of the last hours, exhaustion overcame her and she fell into an uneasy sleep.

Chapter 46

The alarm went off at six thirty and Jed dragged himself into the bathroom, his hands were torn and scratched and there were red marks on his face where the underbrush had caught him. His mum and dad had been out the previous evening and so he'd been spared the need to explain his filthy appearance and his ruined clothes.

Back in the bedroom he retrieved the stained trousers from where he'd flung them in the corner. It was no good, they were only fit for the bin, and so on top of everything else he was going to have to fork out for another business suit. He had planned to buy a new one once he had his commission from The Willows sale, but now the whole thing seemed as shaky as ever, in fact it was even more uncertain if he couldn't put the solicitor in touch with Mrs Carmody. The legal shenanigans could go on for years and Langleys wouldn't keep their offer on the table for ever.

He fished out his second best, now his only work suit, and once dressed he carried the jacket and went down into the kitchen to make a cup of coffee and force down some cereal.

He stepped out pulling the door closed behind him. Striding forward into the growing daylight he straightened his shoulders and lifted his chin. He would fix it today, there was no other option.

At The Willows, the small side gate was closed but not locked and on his way through to the garage area he stopped to peer through the half glazed door into the darkened kitchen. Everything was just the same as before. He glanced at his watch, it was almost quarter past seven, was it too early? He had often met Libby at the bus stop around eight so she must get up about now, and so he carried on across the paved area and the damp grass.

The door at the top of the stairs hung open just as it had the night before and he climbed the familiar concrete steps wary and apprehensive. He knocked just once out of habit and then walked into the deserted flat. Nothing had changed, dirty dishes still sat on the draining board and the bin was beginning to smell as the food inside decayed.

He rubbed a hand over his face, with no idea of what the hell to do next.

He'd seen her over in the woods, so supposed that to be the logical place to start looking. She could have fallen but it was just a little pretend wood, not some dark forest with rocky cliffs and hidden crevices. Still, that was where he had seen her.

It only took a few minutes to get there and it was as he had thought, a bit overgrown in some areas but really just a wooded part of the grounds filled with mixed deciduous trees. He followed the narrow dirt path but it all felt very empty. He knew already that he wasn't going to find Libby here with her foot caught in a rabbit hole or lying under a fallen branch. He could see her footprints though, trodden into the soft earth and, where the woods ended down beside the river, he followed them until they turned up and away over the grass and disappeared. In the absence of any other option he climbed back towards the road which ran along this side of the property. It was a lower wall here than that which ran along the other border. He clambered over the rounded coping stones, to the crumbling edge of the tarmac on a narrow country road. There was a soft grassy edge and tyre marks indicated a car had parked recently, but there was no other sign of life as he trudged back along the road taking him to the big main gates.

It was bright daylight now and he had no idea what to do next. He'd go back into the flat, leave another note. She wasn't missing, not really. He had seen her yesterday after all, so there was no need to contact the police – was there? The abandoned flat was a puzzle though. Perhaps she had just gone, had enough and simply walked away. She had told him that she had done it before. He would go back, look in the cupboards and see if her clothes were there. It was an intrusion into her privacy, of course it was, but he was doing it with the best intentions. If she took offence, so be it.

It felt awkward and uncomfortable, but he walked straight through to the bedroom and pulled open the wardrobe. Of course, he had no reference point but there were certainly clothes there, a couple of the short skirts she wore and two black tops on wire hangers, a few pairs of jeans and a pair of black boots standing on top of a shoe box. He dragged open the integral drawer feeling even more like a weirdo, to find that it was full of underwear, bits of fabric with the odd ribbon and frill of lace, he pushed it closed quickly without touching anything. His face heated as the flush swam up from his neck.

"What the hell do you think you're doing?"

The screech from the doorway had him spinning so fast he tumbled backwards onto the bed floundering on top of the fluffy duvet and knocking the dressing gown to the floor.

"Shit. What the hell, Libby…" He stopped mid-sentence as the skinny dark-haired figure that wasn't Libby took a step into the room.

Chapter 47

"I asked you what you were doing!"

"I was looking for Libby." She raised her eyebrows and leaned to look beyond him. "In the wardrobe?"

"No, of course not. Her clothes, I was checking her clothes."

"So, as I said – what are you doing? Are you supposed to be checking her clothes? What are you, the butler?"

"I'm a friend, just a friend. She's not here."

The woman twisted to one side and then the other. "Hmm, seems not. Have you looked under the bed?" He detected in her shades of Libby. She had the quirkiness and recalcitrance, but underneath there was a bitterness that may be real, or may just seem so as a consequence of the knowledge he had of her.

"Don't be ridiculous. She's missing and I'm concerned for her. Anyway, come to that, who are you and why are you in her place?"

He knew who it was of course, he had known immediately – and all the stories had come flooding back. From close up, she looked like an older and much more ravaged version of Libby. She had the same figure and similar colouring, but her face was sunken at the cheeks and deep lines fanned the outer corners of her eyes. He realised that of course she was the woman seen leaving the antique shop, appearing young to old Mr Taylor, but well into her forties, which was very obvious from close quarters in the daylight. So, this was Sarah. Sarah of the violent temper and the mental problems. It made him awkward and uneasy.

"I'm the owner." Sarah faced him head on.

"No, you're not."

"And how would you know?"

"Mrs Carmody is the owner, she's an old lady."

"I'm her representative and the caretaker is an employee."

"The caretaker?"

"Yes, this Libby who needs you to look through her clothes. She works for me, for us," she said.

Was it really possible that she didn't know who Libby was? "Well she's not here."

"No, she's staying with me."

"What?"

"The caretaker, she's staying with me, she wasn't well and so out of a sense of duty and responsibility I have taken her to stay with me. I came to get some stuff for her and make sure everything was alright."

He was even more confused now. "Libby, the girl who lives here, is staying with you?"

"Yes." She crossed her arms in front of her narrow body and leaned her weight on one hip, confrontational and antagonistic. Jed tried to unscramble the information but it just wouldn't fall in line.

"How long has she been staying with you?"

"Since Wednesday, she was taken ill on Wednesday night."

"But I was with her on Wednesday, she was fine." For just a moment she was wrong-footed and glanced away from him.

"Well it must have been later, she rang me, I came over to see how she was."

"What's wrong with her?"

"A virus, she'll be fine in a day or two. I'll tell her you came over, tell her to ring you when she's better." He wanted to cut through the bullshit, he wanted to call her out on the obvious lie but Libby's stories, tales of violence and uncontrolled behaviour, were getting in the way.

"She hasn't got her phone." He pointed through the door towards where the little handset sat on the kitchen bar.

"No, no she asked me to bring it. I'm taking it with me." Oh, she was good; this woman was a very accomplished liar. Jed raised a hand and rubbed at his jaw. "So, you can go now. She'll be fine."

He was trespassing, this woman had more right than him to be there but it was just so very wrong. If he told her that the 'caretaker' was her daughter, then Libby would probably never forgive him, but why was she pretending that she knew her whereabouts? Maybe just to get him out of the bedsit.

He took a small step towards her. "I'm dealing with the sale."

"Ah, are you from the agents, from Baileys?"

"Bailey and Herriot, yes." He strode towards her now stretching out his hand. "Jed Carlisle, I thought you were away."

"Hmm – I'm back now."

"And Mrs Carmody, is she back? We really do need to speak to her directly."

She took his hand briefly in hers barely touching cold fingers to his palm before drawing back her arm, crossing it tightly with the other across her chest. "Well you can't, that's not possible. As you said, she's an old lady. She's not been well and anyway, I thought it was all sorted out. The house is under offer."

How far should he go now? Mike Irwin had told him about the letter in confidence. "There are a couple of things that just need clarifying. Actually, it's the solicitor really who needs a meeting." This was getting him nowhere. It wasn't helping to find Libby and the deeper he sank into the confusion, the more ridiculous it seemed to keep up the pretence that he didn't know about the mother and daughter relationship.

"Look I'll tell you what, I'd love to have a word with Libby, just to let her know I'm thinking about her, you know, and if you could take me to see her, maybe while we're at it we can contact Mrs Carmody and sort that out as well."

The change was sudden and horrific, she launched herself at him and grabbed at his arms, pulling and tugging, trying to turn him and drive him towards the door. She had a wiry strength and of course he had no way to fight back, he could never have raised a hand against this little female, not even in self-defence. She was hissing at him now.

"Get out, get the hell out. I'm going to ring your superiors. I'm going to tell them all about you, pawing and prowling through people's clothes, being in young women's bedrooms." He had no choice but to move in front of her and cross the lounge to the door. Still she pushed at him, kicking out with her legs, catching him painfully on the calf. "Out, go on, get out." As he stepped over the threshold, she slammed the door behind him leaving him bewildered and worried as he walked back down the steps, desperate now to find Libby.

Chapter 48

Libby was cold, sore and thirsty. She stood and gathered up the limp, brown mass of woollen blanket. She carried it back to where Marian's body lay, ice cold to the touch after the hours that had passed. It felt odd to lay the warm covering on the cold corpse and so she unfolded it in front of her and waved it gently a few times to disperse the residual heat, and then she spread it over her great aunt leaving it to drape down the edge of the hard bench. "There we are, I'm sorry we're still here. I'm goin' to see what I can do now."

She twisted, stretched and jogged on the spot to move her muscles and try to get blood flowing, she rubbed at her arms and blew on her hands. It made little difference; dehydration caused her head to pound and made her feel drugged and sluggish.

Though it was going over old ground she climbed the shallow stairs to the cellar door and kicked out at it in frustration. Thin veins of light crept through where the boards had shrunk. So, it was daytime. For a moment she couldn't remember what day this was and that disturbed her deeply. She leaned against the wood, head lowered and arms wrapped around herself. Wednesday night she had seen Jed and heard the noise and come to investigate. She couldn't have been unconscious for very long after her tumble down the stairs, so that had been the night she had cradled Marian in the cold and the dark. Thursday was the day the old lady had died. She fixed the thought in her memory, it seemed important. So today must be Friday, early or late – it was impossible to know.

She knew that her body desperately needed fluid, but had nothing. She flicked the little lighter and slowly, so that the tiny flame didn't blow out, moved around the space. It didn't cast its light very far and it robbed her of her night vision, so was probably more harm than good.

Before extinguishing it though, she was drawn back to the body lying on what now looked like a bier in an ancient tomb. She bent to look at Marian's face in the flickering light. While they had sat together, Libby giving her aunt body heat and ultimately watching her dying, it had only been a pale oval in the gloom, almost featureless. Now she felt compelled to fix the features in her mind while there was still time. The dull, dead eyes were slightly open and the jaw was gaping. Libby felt guilty that she hadn't thought to make the old lady look better, just as if she was sleeping, as they had done with her dad. When she tried to move the eyelids and jaw it was horrible to find that they were fixed and waxy to the touch. Marian's face was set in rigor mortis and now for the first time the dead body seemed to be a dreadful thing.

Libby stepped back sharply. Her foot sent a small object clattering away. Peering down in the flickering light she saw a water bottle laying on its side close by, dribbling precious water onto the floor. She grabbed it up and lifted it to her lips glugging great mouthfuls until all too quickly the bottle was emptied.

"Bloody hell, Marian, you could have told me."

She addressed the lifeless form more out of bravado than irritation. The more time that passed since the death, the more horrible it became. The gentle drifting away had felt kind in its way but now there was no echo of the old lady, just a cold lifeless carcass. She would pretend she had company and wouldn't look again at the gaunt and gaping face.

With the lighter back in her pocket she waited for her vision to re- adjust, then holding her hands out in front she moved to the wall and sliding her palms up and down and back and forth examined the old bricks for anything that might offer some sort of tool, although exactly what she couldn't have said.

There were hooks fastened to the wall but they were high up and, though it was possible to touch them, she had nothing to lift her to get enough purchase to drag or unscrew them from their anchorage points. She jumped and grabbed out at them but only succeeded in tearing the skin of her fingers and jarring her legs and feet as she let go to fall back to the floor.

In the corner of the old place was a pile of filthy, disintegrating sacks which would be of no use even as covers, she left them and moved on. There were two crumbling wooden boxes in the furthest corner from the body and she slid them away from the wall. She felt around the edges for nails but they were simple things and had been fixed with twisted wire. They came apart easily and she stacked the wood in a small pile. The wire was thin and weak and didn't seem as though it would be of any use as a chisel or makeshift crowbar to use for prying the door frame. But, it might be used to try and pick the lock, though in truth she had no idea how to go about it.

In the back of the door there was a small hole which allowed in a tantalising bead of light; she poked an end of the wire through, right through and out. It wagged and turned but she knew that was pointless. What she had to do was to somehow turn something inside the lock, but what did she know of locks and picks? She drew it back and bent the end; now it looked a bit like the end of a key. She probed into the keyhole with it, twisting and pushing and flicking it back and forth but it was no use, it didn't connect with anything, just rattled and caught on the wood. "Well, Marian, as a burglar I have to say I'm pretty spectacular." She sat back on her heels, it wasn't going to work. She just didn't have the skill.

There had to be something else she could do. Maybe she could attract attention, but as the thought flicked through her mind, she gave a snort of derision, just whose attention was she going to attract? The cellar door was at the side of the house, below ground level in a garden which was hidden behind a high stone wall. The possibility of a passing postman was pretty remote, especially as the post was left in a box next to the main gates. By the time the gardener came she would be in a pretty bad way, she glanced over at the dark hulk. Would the body begin to decay and smell? It must, but how long would that take? She felt a lump rise in her throat and for the first time, allowed the truth to have its place in her mind – that she was in fact, very scared. She tried to push the thought away but this situation was dire and she knew it.

Jed. He had been back and forth and at times she had just wished he'd go away. She'd had to cultivate the friendship, get him to trust her but the more time she had spent with him the more chance there was of letting slip the wrong information. Apart from that she didn't like sharing her space and would have preferred to see him under her own terms, at the bus stop or in the pub but he had turned up over and over. Would he come now? What were the chances?

Ironically, he was now her only hope.

Even if he did come, how would he find her here? He might call at the flat, might even look for her in the big house. She had to make sure that if there was the slightest chance, he would notice the door of the cellar. She went back again to Marian. Old ladies used handkerchiefs, didn't they? She set aside the blanket and lifted the woman's grubby cardigan away from her skinny torso. She pushed her hand into the pocket and found a wadded dirty piece of tissue. So much for that. She needed something light and thin, nothing she wore was pale, light or thin. "Sorry, Marian, I really am, I'll get you a new one, something snazzy for your funeral I promise." And she pulled up the cotton nightdress and tore at it until a long strip of fabric came away in her hand. The movement had disturbed the corpse and she had to push her back onto the makeshift bed and then pull the damaged garment back over the pale arthritic knees.

She pushed the wire through the fabric and back again, then wound it tightly around the handle of her makeshift flag. She took it back to the door only to find that it was far too thick to push through the tiny hole. She slid down with her back against the wood and flung the wire and fabric away across the dark cellar. She had believed herself to be self-reliant, strong and resilient, and now it seemed that an old locked door and her own mother's action were to be her undoing. Her mind was a blank, for the first time in years she felt helpless and hopeless, and tears burned her eyes.

Chapter 49

Jed turned out of the narrow side gate heading for the main road. It was nine o'clock and the morning traffic was increasing. He carried on for a few yards and then stopped. He couldn't just walk away from this. For one thing going into the office with no news wasn't an option, and for another it was obvious that Sarah had lied and lied again. In the bedroom he had been caught off guard, embarrassed and guilty but the things that he had been told didn't make any sense.

He had believed Libby walked through the wood on Thursday evening, but it could just as easily have been Sarah, seen from a distance in the dark – yes, it was probably Sarah.

And what of Mrs Carmody? He was no nearer to finding out where the old lady was.

Perhaps he should report Libby missing. Her clothes were there, and she wasn't. But then he imagined trying to explain to the police about her mother, vanished old ladies, wills and letters – no that wasn't happening. What he could do though was to go into the office, be up front about the whole thing, the covering up that he had done and the obfuscation. He gave a huff and shook his head – he'd be out of a job. Or, instead of standing about like a prat, he could do what he should have been doing – he could go back and find her.

* * *

Libby searched for the wire flag, scrabbling around on the filthy floor. She crawled on her hands and knees until eventually she had it back in her possession. She tore at the fabric again until what was left was a thin streamer fixed to the end of the piece of metal. She wound it as tightly as possible down the full length of the makeshift handle. It was a tight fit but with a final spurt the thing poked through the keyhole and into the light. She shook and juggled it until the fabric unrolled and then jerked it back and forth and felt the pull of it as her flag waved on the outside of the cellar door. She dragged it back a little now and wedged it in the hole. It would do no good to sit all day wagging it back and forth, though in truth there was little else for her to do, but it was there, dangling from the keyhole. She needed to wee and went the noisome place that she had used before and squatted in the dark. She reached out and pulled a piece of the old sacking towards her and used it to wipe herself dry. She felt filthy and knew that she was beginning to smell, there was no help for it.

That done she jogged on the spot until she felt warmer, then went back to the door to sit and listen. There were birds tweeting in the garden, but it was too far away to hear the traffic on the road. She sighed and leaned back against the wood. There must be something else to do. She took up another piece of the wire and began picking at the door with it. It bent and broke but now and then she was rewarded by a sliver of wood splintering away. Maybe if she dug away for long enough, she could weaken the board near to the lock and simply kick it out. Occasionally she jiggled the banner although it seemed pretty futile. Until the light changed. It was so subtle that she would have

189

missed it had she not been concentrating on picking at the boards.

The shadow passed, stealing the gleam of light from the gaps in the wood. Someone was outside, she grabbed the handle and jerked and rattled it frantically, "Hello, I'm in here. Can you hear me? In the cellar. Hello."

She felt the pull on the wire, she pulled back still yelling, thumping now with her other hand. Again, it was pulled, stronger this time, yet stronger and then it was gone. Snatched from her grasp and dragged through the little hole.

Her palm was torn and bleeding, and her other hand was throbbing from thundering on the door. She stood up, pulled at her clothes, fastened her jacket and waited. She waited for the rattle of the key in the lock, waited for the shout from outside telling her it was all okay, she'd be out in a minute. Just hold on. She waited. The shadow moved away. They'd be back in a minute, probably gone to get the key or an axe. She waited.

* * *

Sarah flung the wire flag as far as she could into the flower border and dragged the gate closed behind her. She turned to the left and around the corner to where her little car was parked.

Jed watched her go.

Chapter 50

He started back in the flat. Though she certainly wasn't there it was as good a place as any. All was as he had seen it except for the absence of Sarah screaming and kicking him.

Before he left, he snatched the bunch of keys from the hook by the door and then let himself into the big house by way of the small, half-glazed blue side door. It felt empty; walking around dead rooms and peering into cupboards and storage spaces, he could feel that she wasn't there but was compelled to look anyway. He called her name as he went.

Afterwards he closed and locked the door and then turned to the end of the vegetable garden. A small rickety shed sat against a wall. The dirty little window didn't give much of a view from outside. It looked dusty and neglected inside but when he turned the knob the lock opened smoothly. Old hinges creaked and the door stuck on weeds grown along the edge of the path and it was pretty obvious nobody had been in amongst the old tools and pots for a long time.

There were other outhouses and he would search them all. Why Libby would be in them was a mystery but at least he could then cross them off his mental list. She must after all be somewhere.

Did Sarah actually know? Impossible to even guess, and once he had exhausted the estate what then? Was it possible that Libby had simply gone and he would never see her again? The thought was horrible.

His phone vibrated in his pocket and he groaned pulling it out and reading the screen 'Mike Irwin'. He was surprised by the time notification glowing on the tiny screen – he had been more than an hour in the house and shed. He was very late for work and hadn't let them know. More trouble to deal with. He clicked the accept key.

"Mr Irwin, good morning."

"Jed, I won't keep you, just calling to say thank you."

"Thank you?"

"Yes, for your speedy action regarding The Willows." Best not to speak and so he simply made a small noise, a grunt. "Mrs Carmody's representative came in this morning, about half an hour ago, unfortunately it was before I arrived at the office. I have an appointment with her later. It would have been better of course to meet with Marian immediately but at least we are moving forward so, thank you."

"Right, good. So, I'll join you, shall I?" He had to be there, he just had to be.

"No, no I think better not. It may be necessary for us to discuss other confidential subjects, no better not. I'll keep you informed of course." And with that he rang off.

'Mrs Carmody's representative'? Libby? But why suddenly, and why not let him know first? He had walked back towards the house as he had been speaking and intended to move on to the little workshop and the garage. Should he carry on? If she had contacted Irwin's perhaps it was pointless.

He heard a car draw up on the other side of the wall, quick footsteps on the road and then the creak of the side gate. If this was Sarah, he didn't want her to find him. He jogged back around the corner to where the cellar steps were. The door was below ground level and he could hide there until she had gone. The steps were mossy and damp but the space was shadowed and would serve. He jumped down the small flight and tripped at the bottom. He shot his hands forward to save himself and they thudded against the soggy old wood but he didn't fall. He took a handkerchief out of his pocket to wipe the mess from his hand and then pushed into the corner to wait.

On the other side of the door Libby pressed her ear to the boards. She had heard the dull thump and surely she had felt a thud. She grabbed the metal pick and pushed it through the keyhole, she yelled out, "Hello, help – help. Hello, I'm in here."

The wire poked against Jed's side and the shock sent him back onto the bottom step, his hand against the place on his jacket where he thought he had been attacked. By what? A rat, maybe a cat, something had clawed at him anyway. He scanned the area and that was when he saw it, a shiny stick of some sort jigging back and forth in the keyhole. He turned to look back into the garden but couldn't see much because of the low vantage point. He leaned nearer to the door, trying to keep the noise to a minimum he whispered. "Libby, Libby is that you?"

"Jed, thank god. Yes, I'm locked in. Let me out, for Christ's sake get me out of here."

"Quiet, Libby, just keep quiet. I think Sarah is here. Keep your voice down."

"Bugger that, Jed, just get me out of this place. Marian is in here."

"Marian, do you mean Mrs Carmody? Bloody hell, is she alright?"

"No, she's not soddin' well alright, she's dead. Please, Jed, get me out."

He jumped back up the steps into the garden, he would go to the shed; there must be something there to break the lock or smash the wood of the door. As he turned the corner, Sarah was looking straight at him.

"You again! Why are you back here?"

"Never mind that. Libby is stuck in the cellar and Mrs Carmody is down there, she's dead."

Chapter 51

Jed tried to move on, intent on reaching the shed, finding something to use to release Libby. Sarah stepped in front of him. He shifted to the side, and tried to get around her.

"Didn't you hear me? Libby is locked in the cellar and Mrs Carmody is dead. Get out of the bloody way."

Sarah shifted again, blocking his way. "No, she's not, she's not dead and anyway, what has any of this to do with you?" The question brought him up short.

He'd had enough.

"Libby is Elizabeth, your daughter, and she's locked in the cellar with Mrs Carmody your aunt, who it seems, is dead. Is that clear enough for you?"

Sarah shook her head then leaned and looked past him in the direction of the cellar. "This is nothing to do with you. You're only supposed to be selling the house, that's all you have to do. I don't know why you think you can come round here trying to take over."

Jed bent towards her, he grasped her upper arms, forcing her to look at him, "I'll say it again. Elizabeth, your daughter, is down in the cellar with the dead body of your aunt. Now, move and let me get some tools and let her out."

He pushed her sideways and she stumbled, causing him to grab out at her again and hold her more tightly. She muttered to herself quietly, and closed her eyes. When she opened them again, she looked perplexed.

"Marian can't die yet. She can't die until it's all over. When it's all gone and she has nothing left, but not yet. I have to go and see the solicitor. No, she can't die yet. I've brought her some food," she said.

She held up a thin carrier bag, there was a bottle of water sagging against the side and Jed could see a small triangular package – a sandwich maybe. The story began to fall into place, it was incredible but everything started to make a sort of insane sense. "You. Was it you? You locked them in?"

"I had to, I had to get her out of the way. It was your fault though," she said pointing at him and nodding, "insisting I unlock her room. She'd have been okay in there." She pointed at the house. "She'd been fine in there for ages, sleeping in her own dirt and so grateful for all the help we gave her. Stupid old woman. I had her under control. I'd kept her quiet. We'd even washed her, cleared away her stink, cut her hair. Didn't I keep her quiet? But no, not enough for you, was it? You insisted that the room was opened. And then I received an email – 'Oh you have to let me into the room, you have to, they need access. You have to take her to live with you.' Well, that wasn't happening, no, why should I have to look after her, run around waiting on her hand and foot. No thank you, anyway she was alright, she had a mattress. I came to see her."

Now she tipped a head to one side, a frown wrinkled the skin between her eyes, deepening the groove.

"This should have been my place. You do understand that, don't you? And even though Elizabeth left me, she ran off and left me on my own. I was willing to share with her, but she's so bossy. Never mind, I'll let her out, when it's all sorted out. I'll let her out. You have to let me past. I have to go and take this to Aunt Marian." She lifted the bag, and shook it in front of him. "I have to give her the water and some more medicine, can't have her waking up. When it's all done, when I've seen the solicitor and it's all mine, then she can die. But not until she feels it, feels what it's like to have nothing." She tried to push past him, but Jed held her back.

"My God, has it been you, all of this? The house sale, the paperwork, everything? And all this time, that poor woman was locked up?"

"Well of course silly, who else would it be? There is nobody else, they're all dead. Mummy and Daddy – they drowned, and then Brian, all gone. Nobody left, just her, the old bitch and she can die now, once I've shown her what it was like. What it feels like to have nothing."

"Have you got the cellar key?" She pulled it from her pocket, a big old fashioned brass key with a long shaft and a heavy bit. She wagged it in front of him and as he reached to snatch it from her, she danced backwards along the path.

"Oh no, you can't have it. I have to go and give her some water and then I have to lock her up again, it's nearly over. It's taken a lot of planning but it's nearly over now. She can come out when it's all done. I'll let Elizabeth out then, when she can't interfere any more, can't try and control everything. It's all going to be fine."

She was mad, wasn't she? This little woman, older version of wacky, fascinating Libby, she was quite mad. He felt completely unprepared for this, had no idea how to proceed.

"No, Sarah, you have to give me the key and you have to let me go and get them out. After that we can talk. You can talk to her, your daughter, Libby – Elizabeth. You'd like that wouldn't you? Wouldn't you like to see your daughter?"

"No."

"But, it's your little girl."

"She always tried to bully me, she always has. Once my Brian died, she thought she could take over but no, I'm her mother after all. It should be me that makes the decisions."

"Christ, you pushed her down the steps? How could you? And then you locked her in, with a dying woman?"

"Well she would have been angry, she kept saying we had to wait, wait and wait but my way is so much better, so much cleverer. She'd be angry, I know she would, she's always getting angry." She shook her head, "It runs in the family I'm afraid, it's not her fault but it was the only thing to do. It used to work when she was small, she didn't like the dark. She soon behaved herself when I told her I'd lock her in the cupboard. She got over it though, she always got over it." She sighed now and looked up at him her mouth turned down and her eyes wide and sorrowful. "Don't worry though, I'll let them both out once the house is sold and the money is in my bank account. You should go, you should tell that solicitor to get a move on, tell him that it's all okay and he must just do as he's told. Then they can come out. When it's all gone."

In the background, like distant thunder he could hear Libby pounding on the cellar door.

Chapter 52

Jed changed tack. "Here, let me have that bag. I'll carry it for you, we can go together and take it to Marian. I'll help you." He needed to get down there, to let Libby out and see what had really happened to Mrs Carmody. He reached out and took the plastic carrier. To his surprise Sarah gave it up easily and linked her arm through his.

"Well thank you so much." They stumbled along the narrow path and then down the first of the dingy steps. He called out, "It's okay, Libby, we're here. It's okay."

"Well you took your time. Come on, bloody well get me out." Sarah tutted as she shook her head and then turned to take the shopping from his hands. "Now, you have to wait here, and then we'll go and see the solicitor." In her twisted world all was in order, she was in control.

She inserted the key into the old lock, turned it and began to pull the door but it flew open knocking her onto the dirty concrete slab. Libby pushed through the space and stumbled on the flailing feet of her mother who was scrabbling backwards up the steps.

"What the hell? Shit, Mum it's you!"

Jed leaned forward, he dragged the older woman to her feet and reached out a hand to Libby who was standing in

the doorway watching in disbelief as her mother
straightened her clothes and picked up the fallen carrier
bag. She turned to Jed, "Where did she come from?"

"She was in the garden, coming to see to Marian."

"Well, she's come too bloody late, by a long way. She's
in there, dead and cold. Do you know what you've done?"
She had grabbed hold of Sarah's face, one hand on each
side of her head, she was peering close into her eyes. "Do
you understand what you've done now? She's dead."

"No, no she can't be," Sarah shook her off and stepped
towards the cellar door. "She can't die yet."

Libby turned to Jed, "I think you have to call the
police. We need the police and I suppose an ambulance."

"Are you alright, Libby?"

"Me? Well yeah, I smell like a stable and I'm thirsty but
yeah, I'm okay. Marian though, she's in there. She just
drifted off in the end, in the stinking cellar, in the dark."

"You were with her then, when she died, you were
there?"

"Yes, we were trying to keep warm."

"That must have been horrible."

"Well, it wasn't the best way to spend a night." She
shrugged him off, turned and followed the sound of
Sarah's voice. While they had been talking, she had shoved
past them.

Jed took out his phone, turned on the torch. They
heard the sobbing before they could see round to where
the body lay against the wall. At first it seemed that Sarah
was overwhelmed with grief, she sobbed and groaned.
Libby turned and looked at him and raised her eyebrows
and then they drew nearer.

"Stop it, stop it – Mum, leave her!" She dashed forward
and began struggling with the other woman, who was
holding the dead body in what had at first seemed to be an
embrace. Sarah was trying to pull the corpse from the thin
damp mattress, she was trying to make it stand. "You're
not dead, you're not. You can't be dead. It's not time. Stop

it now, stop pretending. You can't be dead." They ran to where Sarah struggled to hitch the heavy weight upwards. Jed grabbed at her, dragging her away and Libby threw herself towards the body of her great aunt as it slid hideously towards the floor.

"Bloody hell! Stop it, Sarah. Leave her, she's dead. Can't you see it's too late? She's dead. It's all over, leave her now. Let Elizabeth cover her up. We need to get an ambulance for her. Just leave her." She spun from his grasp and backed away shaking her head and pointing.

"No, that's not fair, I wanted her to know what it's like, to feel the despair. She can't have it her way, she always had it her way, they all did. No." She turned and before he could stop her, she ran for the door, up the steps and out into the garden. Libby had turned and clattered up the steps grabbing out at Sarah's clothes.

"I'll catch her, Jed, go and see to Marian."

He crossed the cellar. Marian's body was sprawling half on and half off the shelf. He lifted her legs and, fighting back the wave of nausea, he slid her onto the mattress and dragged the blanket back up and over the corpse.

He jogged up the steps into the bright day and looked around but the women had vanished. "Libby, where are you? Libby, Sarah, come back. It's okay. It's all going to be okay!"

He dashed back through the produce garden expecting that Sarah would head for the car parked outside, but the gate was closed. He turned and ran back to the front of the house. There they were. Sarah had, crossed the drive and was now running onto the grassy meadow leading to the wood and the lake, Libby was just yards behind her and he heard her frantic shouts, "Mum, mum! It's alright, come back. We'll help you."

He glanced back, hesitated for just a moment but Marian was dead, Libby needed help, he joined the mad race. They sped on, Sarah's long cardigan flying behind her, on and on pounding down to the lake and wood. If

she made it through the trees she could be over the low
wall and away, but as he watched she veered to the left and
slipped and slithered down the increasing slope towards
the glinting water.

"Wait, Libby, Sarah – wait!"

Chapter 53

Because of the slope of the ground, Jed lost sight of the two women, but he ran on gasping and desperate. The next time he saw them they were clambering on the rocks at the narrow end of the expanse of water, the place where he had seen Libby crying. She had almost caught up with her mother and he stopped for a moment to catch his breath. He was bent at the waist, his hands braced against his thighs, lungs burning and throat on fire. He heard the splash, when he lifted his head all he saw was Libby standing on the rocks, her arms by her sides and her body leaning towards the water.

"Where is she? Can you see her?" he shouted.

"She's here. She's in the lake." He had reached the bank now and scanned the surface but Sarah had vanished.

"I can't see her." Libby was alongside him now a hand to her brow, her head turning frantically back and forth. "She was on the rocks. I almost had her." When Jed reached out to take her hand, Libby didn't pull back as she might have done before. He looked down and saw his own fear reflected in her face, there was nothing he could say to reassure her.

They slithered and stumbled down the bank. "Be careful, Libby, it's slippery."

"She's scared of water."

"What?"

"Terrified of the water, always has been, after what happened. She can't swim, neither of us can swim."

"There!" Jed pointed towards the centre of the lake. Sarah must have submerged as she went in and now bobbed to the surface yards from the rocks and swept by the current, rolling and swirling towards the huge grating in front of the drainage pipe. "It's okay, it's okay. Stay here." Libby was staring at her mother as the water carried her on. Her eyes were pools of horror, dirty fingers covered her mouth. She glanced at Jed, then turned back to the lake and walked as far as she could, up to her ankles in the shallow water licking at the muddy bank.

Jed kicked off his shoes as he ran and then plunged down past Libby, he shrugged out of his jacket and dragged his trousers down and over his feet, and then he forged forward. As soon as it was deep enough, he thrust off with his legs, his arms reaching. His crawl stroke was strong, he'd swum for the school and county and had always loved being in the water, but the pull of the current was stronger, dragging at him and it scared him. He tried to adjust and keep some control but Sarah was struggling in the middle of the lake, her arms flailing, the pale blob of her face vanishing over and over as the water took her under. Libby was yelling from the bank; it sounded muted and distant. "Mum, Mum, hang on. He'll get you."

It spurred him on. He gave up some of the attempt at control and let the rush of water carry him. He was bumped and knocked by floating debris but the flow swept him towards where Sarah was. He struggled to keep her in his sights because she was sinking more and more often now.

Libby called from the bank, "She's gone, Jed, I can't see her, it's no good, she's gone."

He took in three deep breaths, exhaling between to make sure his lungs expanded fully and then duck-dived into the murky depths. Visibility was very poor. The lake was full of leaves and twigs and though the water itself was clear it was dark with swirling sediment; he could only see a few inches in front of his face. He pulled back up to the surface, spun his head and caught a glimpse of the pale cardigan a few yards to his left. As he swam towards her Sarah vanished again and he dived under. Legs kicking, arms stretching, he pulled with all his strength as he tried to reach her. She was no longer struggling but swirling downwards just an arm's length away. He kicked out and reached, grabbing at her clothes. His finger ends touched the fabric but as he tried to close his grip she rolled, and it was whisked away from him. His lungs were aching now, his throat beginning to burn but he knew that if he went back to the surface it would be too late, she would disappear into the dark.

He jack-knifed, pushed downwards with his upper body, flicked his legs upwards and kicked hard, going deeper, fighting the current, trying to get underneath her. He caught hold of her hair, twisting it around his right hand and then snatched at her clothes with his left. Now, with his lungs on fire he turned his head to the surface and saw the distant, vague gleam of light on the wavelets above him.

He propelled himself upwards, dragging the dead weight and broke the surface just inches from the pipe. It was too late to avoid it and as his body was slammed into the metal grating he tried to take a stronger hold of the woman but still only held her with one hand in her hair. The relentless rush smashed her, a broken doll against the metal struts. He was desperately trying to keep her face above the surface and his arm and shoulder screamed with the effort. He needed to take in air but the pounding water filled his nose and mouth and he felt his throat close.

He turned away from the flow, threw back his head and coughed and spluttered, snot and water running from his nostrils, but he was able to take in a breath. Sarah was beside him pushed and twisted by the constant gush. He took a great gasp and then spun back round, his back against the grating. The water battered and pounded at him but he was able to use the force of it to hold him in place with his feet twisted between the bars and his legs braced against the metal so that he could wrap a hand around the sagging body. Once he had a better grip, he thrust away from the pipe sideways, at an angle away from the rush of water and kicked with all his remaining strength for the shallows.

As the force decreased, he rolled and wrapped an arm over Sarah. Holding her on his chest and belly as he kicked with his legs to the nearest bank. It was muddy, slimy and steep and all he could do was lean against it, gasping and coughing. He wasn't going to be able to climb out just yet, but the current was weak here and so he half-swam, half-waded until the slope lessened enough for him to scramble out, pushing and dragging the ungainly, helpless body with him.

Chapter 54

Staggering and slipping he struggled up to firmer ground. Sarah hadn't made a sound and her head lolled loosely on her neck as he dragged her with him. Her limbs flopped pathetically on the grass. He laid her on her front, lifted her with a hand under her belly so that her head was lowered and he thumped her back, nothing happened. He flipped her over, laid her straight and tipped her head back, straightening her airway. With his thumb on her chin, he pulled open her mouth and peered inside, there was no obstruction. He tipped her head back and then covered her lips with his own and breathed into her. He drew back, turned to the side, gulped in another breath and again lowered his face to hers, and then again watching her chest, desperately hoping for spontaneous movement.

He was peripherally aware of Libby running round the lakeside. He put his fingers on the side of Sarah's throat, searching for the throb of life and felt only cold, wet skin. He knelt more upright, crossed his hands on her chest and pumped, thud, thud, thud, counting under his breath, one, two, three. Now the breathing, now the pumping, again the breathing and still there was nothing. Again, he pumped her chest. Libby had reached them.

"Kneel down here, Libby. When I tell you – do this," he said as he demonstrated the cardiac massage. "Can you do that? You need to push harder than you want to, don't worry, nice and regular but good and hard." She nodded and crossed her hands on her mother's body.

Thumping, breathing, thumping, breathing and hoping for a sign of life, for the gasp and cough that would tell them that she lived.

There was nothing. On and on. Still there was nothing.

They didn't hear the rush of water, nothing of the song of the birds; all there was in the world was the rhythmic blow of air and the gasp from Libby with each thump of her hands on the still, unresponsive body. On and on they went, willing her to live, to breathe, to reward them with a spurt of watery vomit and the splutter of revival, but it didn't come.

Her lips were blue, Jed pulled up her lids and looked into her eyes, they seemed to him devoid of the light of life but how could he be sure? How did he know whether he should stop? Maybe she was on the verge of recovery. He looked up at Libby, though there were tears forming in her eyes she didn't flinch from his gaze. She shook her head, but he told her, "We should carry on. I think we should." He turned his head again and took in a deep breath but when he bent towards Sarah, he saw that Libby had placed her fingers over her mother's mouth.

"Libby."

She shook her head. "I don't think it's any good. You tried, Jed, we tried, but I don't think it's any good. Leave her now, let her go. I'll go and get the phone. Will you stay with her?"

"I don't know, Libby, we should keep on. We should keep on until an ambulance gets here. You go call the ambulance."

"No, come on now. Leave her, it's over."

He fell back to sit on the grass, his shirt was torn and stuck to him in clammy patches, his arms and legs were suddenly weak and he began to shake and shiver. He nodded and as Libby left to fetch his jacket and to ring for the police and an ambulance, he lowered his head to his bent knees and closed his eyes…

He felt the sudden warmth as his jacket was draped around his shivering shoulders and he looked up into Libby's eyes. Shock had whitened her face, but there were no tears and as she flopped down on the grass beside him to tell him that the police and ambulance were on the way, her voice was steady. She leaned and laid her hand over his.

"You did your best. That was so bloody brave, going into the lake like that. You did your best, Jed." She moved closer and wrapped her arms around him. "You're frozen, here we go. You'll have to ignore the stink, I know I honk a bit but I'm pretty good at sharing body heat."

"I'm sorry, Libby, I'm so sorry."

"Yeah, me too." And they sat together and listened to the wail of the sirens drawing nearer.

* * *

The first responders pounded around the edge of the lake; they brought their defibrillator and oxygen; they went through the motions but everyone knew that it was too late. Sarah was dead, there was to be no bringing her back.

"I'll go and open the main gates, for the ambulance." Libby stood now as the paramedic wrapped Jed in a survival blanket and laid another over Sarah's body.

"Are you sure love, I can do that if you want?" She shook her head and strode away. "Tough your girl, isn't she? Holding it together."

"Oh, she's not my…" Jed stopped himself, it didn't matter. "Yeah, she's awesome. Do you know about the other woman?"

"The other woman?"

"Yeah in the cellar, back at the house." He could tell by the look on the young man's face that either Libby had forgotten to mention about Marian in the drama with Sarah, or the message had become confused. He suddenly felt dreadfully weary and almost didn't bother to go on but with a sigh he continued.

"In the cellar, the woman who owns this place, she's dead." As the emergency worker jumped to his feet grabbing at his bag, Jed held out a hand, "No, she is very dead. She's been dead for a while. Actually, I think you should call the police, unless they are already coming. Shit, what the hell has happened?"

He lowered his head again. He heard the paramedic muttering into his phone and then tuned it all out, listened to the sound of the wind in the trees and the sound of water as it made its way back to the river, and he waited for Libby to come back. Perhaps she would put her arms around him again – he could only hope.

Chapter 55

They insisted on taking Jed to the hospital, and asked Libby if she wanted to go with him in the ambulance. "No, I think I'll just stay here, see what happens with Marian. I'll see you later, Jed, okay?"

"Okay, but let me know what's going on, won't you? Use the phone." His mind was reeling, it had all happened so quickly and now when he tried to replay the parts that made up the whole of the horror, it wouldn't make sense. The conversation in the garden had been surreal and he needed to speak to Libby, needed her to tell him it wasn't true. Of course, her mother had been mad, so nothing she had said could be relied upon, it just needed to be explained that was all.

"Course I will." Then to the obvious surprise of the paramedics she turned and walked towards the little woodland, dragging a smoke from her pocket as she went. Jed gave a small laugh.

"She handles things in her own way. She's great though, really." They shrugged and glanced at each other as they helped him climb into the back of the ambulance which was also going to carry Sarah's poor drowned body to the hospital. He'd told them it wouldn't upset him, and it made things easier.

As they drove through the main gates, they had to pull to one side to let yet another police car through. The whole area was full of uniforms and cars, and Jed would have liked to climb out of the emergency vehicle, find Libby and sit with her in the peace of the woods. But his clothes were wet, he was bruised and sore and his shoulder was on fire. They thought he might have damaged some tendons, so he sat with the shrouded body of her mother and let others take charge.

* * *

"So, where are you now, Jed? I tried to ring but it just kept saying leave a message."

"I had to turn the phone off in the hospital. Did you leave a message?"

"No, I didn't leave a message. Why would I want to do that?"

"Then I would have known that you'd called. I didn't know you had called." He realised that he hadn't actually checked his call log and felt a pang of guilt.

"Yeah, well I said I would. Are you okay anyway, your arm and everything?"

"It's not bad, I've got a sling on and I have to be careful but it's okay, I've got painkillers. Have you been to erm, you know, to see your mum, her body?"

"Not yet. I wondered actually if you'd come with me. It's okay if you're busy or whatever."

"Of course, I'll come. When do you want to do that?"

"Oh shit, I don't know. The police have had me in an interview place for ages, I only just got out. Then they asked me to go and identify Marian, that was stupid as well, I mean I never knew her, did I? Anyway, they seemed to think I was the best one to do it. I said they should get that solicitor bloke but it's done now anyway. I had to go, and just say yes, I was with her when she died and she told me who she was. It was all a bit weird. Anyway, now they have to do a post-mortem on the poor old thing. Christ you'd think she'd been through enough. They know why she died, she was locked in that cellar, she was old – of course she died."

"Well, just tell me and I'll pick you up, I can borrow my mum's car, oh hang on I can't drive, not with my arm in a sling. Never mind I'll work it out. I'll come to the side gate yeah?"

"Yeah well, I'm not there."

"What? How do you mean?"

"I couldn't stay at the flat. The police were everywhere and going through the house and my place. They said I should stay somewhere else for a while. It's all confused right now."

"But where are you?"

"I found a hostel."

"Bloody hell, Libby, you can't stay in a hostel. Not after everything you've been through."

"It's okay, I've stayed in worse places. I'll just meet you in The Feathers, okay? In an hour."

* * *

She was sitting in the window with a pint of lager on the table in front of her. She grinned at Jed as he came up to join her. "Do you want a drink?"

"I'll get it, I can't drink because of the pills but I'll have a coke," he indicated the half empty glass, "Another one?"

"No, better not. It won't look so good if I turn up stinking of booze. At least they let me have a shower at the bedsit. I was sorry about that, I liked living there." She shrugged, yet again accepting the vagaries of her fate.

He had to do it, he had to do it now, have the conversation that would set his mind at rest. He coughed and looked up at her, pale and battered staring at him across the table. Again, he held his tongue.

213

"Right. Listen, Libby, my mum is going to come in the car and run us to the hospital, if that's okay? I'll just ring her when you're ready."

"Okay, that's nice of her."

"Yeah, she's great. Freaked her out a bit when the police turned up at the door to say I was hurt, but she's calmed down now. The thing is though, I told her about you, about where you said you were going to stay." He saw the flare in her eyes, the tightening around her mouth. "Oh, come on, Libby, after what had happened what did you expect? I told her all about it, of course I did. It's what families do."

She lowered her eyes to the table. Her fingers were wrapped around the glass and she slid it backwards and forwards in tiny jerky movements.

"Yeah, well I don't have much experience of that do I?"

"No, I know." He leaned and put his hand on top of hers. "My mum said that if you like you can come and stay with us." Almost before he finished speaking, Libby was shaking her head. "No, just wait, don't say no straight off like that. Please Libby."

"I don't stay with people, Jed. I need to be on my own. I can't. Tell your mum thanks but I'm better on my own."

"But Libby, we've got a spare room, you can even have your own key and come and go as you like. It's nice, Libby, and comfortable, you could stay in the room or join in with us, whatever you like. I just hate it, the idea of you in a hostel. I want to look…" He stopped as she raised her eyes to his. "Shit, Libby, we're friends, aren't we? I just want you to be okay. I want you to be comfortable and safe. Just until you get sorted that's all. Please."

She didn't speak for a long time but then she looked up at him. "Tell you what. If your mum will let me pay her some rent. If I can just be by myself when I want, if I don't have to, you know…"

"I can guess what she'll say about the rent, she's not going to like that…"

"Well." She shrugged and went back to sliding the glass on the wet table.

"Okay. Okay I'll talk to her, will you come though?" She grinned at him.

"Thank you. That'd be great." He sat back on the straight wooden chair, a small glow of happiness had begun deep inside, he pushed it down, all she had agreed to was to come and lodge with them. Still, it was something.

Chapter 56

Sarah looked peaceful, lying in the chapel at the hospital. There was a candle burning on a shelf high on the wall and a white sheet draped across her. Libby stood looking down at her mother; Jed had taken a step back, given her space. She shook her head and turned away.

"I suppose I'll have to sort out a funeral. I don't know if there's any money, I haven't got any. She was living in a rented room and hired that car. Last time I was living with her, it was in a nasty little flat down near London. Just scraping by really, I suppose she still is – was." She sighed and frowned. "I wonder what you do when there's no money. I mean, when my dad died, we managed – some money had been coming in and then the blokes on the site he was on had a whip-round. It just worked out but I don't know how to do this." She turned around and said, "Do you know? No of course you don't. You don't have to worry about stuff like this do you?"

Jed thought about the conversation with Mike Irwin, the revelations about the will and the letter. He didn't know if this was the right time to tell her, to let her know that these were no longer her problems.

"Have you spoken to the solicitor, Libby? Irwin, your Aunt Marian's legal bloke."

"No, I suppose I'll have to, do you think he'll arrange things for her, or is that on me as well? I don't know whether I need to do that. Oh, I see… Ah you think that maybe because she's family. Oh brilliant, that's brilliant Jed. Of course, maybe I can get them to pay. Brilliant."

She beamed at him. He tried to summon up a smile but his spirit had lowered yet more with the comment about where her mother had been living. How did she know where she had been living? She came towards him and stood close, she tipped her head back and looked into his face.

"I need to say this, Jed, thank you for what you did. You were so brilliant at the lake and although, this," she said, as she turned back to the bier holding Sarah, "this is what happened, I'll never forget what you did, the way you tried." She leaned up and kissed him softly on the lips. "Thank you. She was sick and she was nasty and violent but it wasn't her fault, not really and she didn't deserve this. Although, I suppose at the end of the day maybe, just maybe it's better than her being locked up for years and I guess that's what they would have done."

She stopped for a moment and turned, took a step towards her mother's body. "What do you think, Jed, honestly what do you think happened?" He had dreaded this question and struggled to form an answer to have ready, but in the end, he was simple and honest.

"I don't know, I truly don't, she might have slipped, I didn't see but she might have gone in deliberately. She was climbing on the rocks when I last saw her, very near the edge. It's odd though, if she was scared of water why did she go there? Why not run for the woods and get away? Something took her there, to the lake. We'll never know though, will we?"

"I guess it doesn't really matter but I'll always wonder and I have to just find a way to live with that."

Again, the chance to speak passed him by, he couldn't do it here, not in this quiet, reverential place and so he waited and held on to the misery.

They stayed a while longer, sitting on straight back chairs, not really sure what they were supposed to be doing or feeling, but nervous of leaving too soon in case it seemed disrespectful. Then Libby leaned over and in a low voice she said, "Come on let's go. We can't do anything here. Let's just go. I'm whacked and I could do with something to eat. Do you think your mum will think I'm awful if we get a double pepperoni pizza and some garlic bread?"

"She'd only think you're awful if you don't get enough for her as well."

"Come on then. Oh…"

"What?"

"Have you got any money? I forgot to get some from the machine."

* * *

Once they were home and his parents had moved into the living room, giving them space he turned his dining chair so that he was facing her head on. "I spoke to your mum for a little while in the garden, Libby. Before I managed to get the key from her."

"Right."

"She was ranting a bit, already overwrought. She said some stuff though and I wonder if we can talk about it." She shook her head and looked down at the table, fiddling with the handle of her fork.

"Well, you can't really take any notice of anything she might have said then can you, I mean she was clearly out of it wasn't she."

"But the things she said were odd, they didn't make any sense."

"Oh well there you are then. Best to forget about them eh. I might just go out now, go and have a smoke."

"No, Libby, wait. I really think we should talk about this." She sighed and twitched her shoulders.

"Oh, bloody hell, okay then go on."

"She said that you knew what was happening, with Marian. She said that you had been trying to bully her about it."

"Did she, right well as I say, she was deranged wasn't she. Of course, I didn't know. I wouldn't have left her there, in that horrible cellar. I couldn't have done that. Bloody hell, do you really think I could have done that?"

"You told me that she didn't know it was you who was the caretaker, that you did everything through an agency, you said you didn't even know where she was." He sat quietly now, waiting for her to answer him, to put him at ease. "But then earlier today, at the hospital. It sounded as though you knew where she was living?"

"Well, you know, the police must have told me I suppose. I don't know it's all confusing isn't it. Anyway, really does it matter now? She didn't know truth from fiction, did she? Just let it go, Jed. It's all been a mess, just let it go."

He left it because to take it further would lead him into a darkness that he couldn't face but it ate at him, made him ill-tempered and snappy and they avoided each other. Libby stayed in her room most of the time and Jed took long walks while his worried mother watched and wondered what had gone wrong.

It was an odd few days, they moved through it step by step. They felt suspended, isolated from the everyday whilst waiting for the results of the post-mortem on Marian and a date for the inquest.

The police were keeping them informed, but with both women dead it seemed that nothing would be rushed. It was set to go on for a while. Jed's mum had made Libby promise that she would stay with them until it was resolved, until she knew what she was going to do next.

Charles Herriot came to the house. He had heard part of the story and was obviously itching to hear all about it but didn't want to appear to gossip.

"Very strange situation, Jed?"

"Yes, all very complicated, sir."

"You acquitted yourself well though, from the little I've heard. Well done."

"It was all instinct really, Scouts and swimming training, it just all came back. Didn't do much good in the end though."

"No, of course, a sad outcome. Tragic. And Mrs Carmody, all that time locked up and nobody knowing she was there. Well, that's all very odd."

"Yes." Jed nodded and feigned a yawn as the familiar doubt crept back to the surface. He couldn't talk about it, didn't even want to think about it but he knew that it was cowardice, and in the end, it would come to a head.

"Right well you must be tired, I'll be on my way. You take your time now, Jed, don't rush back. Wait until you're ready, fully fit and all that. Of course, everything's on hold with The Willows, bit of a mess there I'm afraid. Place was crawling with police when I drove by yesterday. Not sure what the situation is right now. We might still be able to rescue something. You never know. Mike Irwin's been in touch. Apparently, there's an heir, so maybe it'll still come through. We'll have to wait and see, fingers crossed and all that."

"Yes, sir, fingers crossed."

He really didn't care. It had all become so very secondary. As his mother showed Charles out, he heard Libby's voice in the hall. She had been out for a walk, and he supposed for her smoke. She was being introduced to his boss simply as a house guest and it amused Jed to think that Charles had no idea who he was talking to.

Another voice joined the chatter in the hallway and Libby led one of the policemen who was dealing with the whole mess into the sitting room.

"Oh, hello. I'll just…" he turned to leave but Libby moved to block his way and put a hand on his chest.

"He can stay, can't he?" she asked the policeman.

"Yes, if you're happy with him being here, of course. I just wanted to bring you up to date, let you know where we're at, and we have a few questions for you if that's okay." She nodded and lowered herself onto the sofa. A police woman in uniform had followed the plain clothes detective into the room, she stood quietly near the door, her hat in her hand and her expression bland.

"Right, well, as you know we've been searching the house and grounds trying to piece things together. Because the house had been cleaned and re-organised ready for the viewings, we don't think that we're going to find much in the room that you tell us was locked. But, at the end of the day we are fairly sure that we know what happened – with your statement and the evidence in the cellar. We have to wait for the results of tests and what have you to confirm it but…" He paused for a moment, "We found a large quantity of drugs, a very large quantity hidden in the kitchen and the dining room. We are tending towards the belief that erm…" He coughed, awkward and uncomfortable.

"Sarah…" Libby rescued him. "My mum, it's okay I know she was sick, unbalanced. You don't have to sugar coat things, just say what you have to."

"Right, good, well. It seems pretty clear that she, your mum, had been drugging Mrs Carmody to control her."

"We know all this; we were there weren't we?" Jed reached over and squeezed her hand. "Sorry, sorry it's just, you know, we lived this."

"Don't apologise, I'm just trying to put things in perspective." The policeman smiled and peace was restored. "Anyway, the main thing is that we have found the drugs. We did find a large number of marijuana plants in an old greenhouse which doesn't quite fit with the other drugs which were pharmaceuticals but, well who knows what she was planning with those." Jed squeezed Libby's fingers, they didn't dare look at each other.

"Yes, but as I say we don't know what she was planning with those. They have been destroyed now."

"Oh right, good. In that old greenhouse. Shit." She nodded her head and forced her face into a suitable expression.

"There is another issue though that we need to clarify." He leaned to his briefcase and took out a sheaf of A4 papers. "These," he said, placing the papers face down on the coffee table, "are print outs from the lap top that we found in your own apartment."

Libby leapt to her feet. "What do you mean, what the hell! Have you been through my stuff, through all my stuff?"

"Yes, of course in a situation like this the investigation has to be thorough. Two women are dead we have to get to the truth."

"But you had no right, you didn't. You had no right – Jed." She turned to him and he was shocked by the panic on her face. The policewoman stepped forward, glanced at her boss who raised his hand, holding her back.

"It's okay, Libby, don't get upset. Hang on, just let's find out what this is about." He turned back to the detective, raised his eyebrows.

"There are messages in the email folders that have us puzzled, Libby."

"I deleted all my emails."

"Why did you do that?"

"I'm a tidy freak, I hate old stuff hanging about, I just do, that's all, so there can't be anything. What is this, don't you think I've been upset enough without your attitude, this – this!" She pointed to the paperwork.

"I'm sure you know that almost anything that has been on a computer can be retrieved."

She shook her head. Jed knew that though she had enough knowledge to use the computer and the internet, her skills weren't that great. He also knew by her reaction that there was something on that machine that she hadn't wanted anyone to see. Bile rose in his throat as she flopped back into her seat and pulled out a piece of tissue to wipe at her palms.

"There is stuff on here indicating that in fact you did know that there was someone locked in the room at The Willows. Not only did you know, but that you were complicit in holding her."

"No, that's not true." Her head twisted back and forth between them. "It's not true, it's not. She did it, she locked her up, kept her quiet, she did it. She did it and now she's dead. She fell into that bloody lake and drowned. You saw Jed, you saw what happened, tell them."

Jed felt his heart lurch but he spoke up now. "Libby, I don't think you should say anything else. I think you should get a solicitor."

"I don't need one, no, no – I didn't do anything to that old lady. I tried to help her, in the cellar I kept her warm."

Jed reached out, desperate to keep her calm. She spun to face him, pointing a shaking finger.

"If anyone here's to blame it's you. Yeah, you should take some of the blame."

"Me!"

"Yeah, you. You were the one who caused her to be moved. You were the one who insisted that the room was opened."

"Bloody hell, Libby, don't you think if I'd have known for even one second, don't you think I would have got her help. Shit, I know I did some pretty stupid stuff but…"

The policeman had gathered the papers together and stood. "I don't think either of you should say any more, not until we have this on a formal footing."

"But… I didn't know. Christ you can't think I knew anything about this." Jed felt tears of panic fill his eyes. "I didn't know."

Chapter 57

Jed spent uncomfortable and nerve-wracking hours in a dingy room at the police station.

They were polite, thoughtful even. They brought him drinks and asked him repeatedly if he needed painkillers for his arm. But they questioned him extensively. He refused a solicitor. It was a bridge too far and it would make him look as though he had something to hide.

"Why did you agree to conduct business with a go-between?"

"It was the only way they would agree to do it."

"Did you never suspect that Mrs Carmody was imprisoned, you viewed the property, took pictures, measurements."

"Yes, but the room was locked?"

"Didn't that seem odd to you?"

"Well of course but Libby said it had always been locked."

"And you had no idea there was someone in there, someone being held against their will?"

"No, no of course I didn't, God do you really think I would have left her there." There was no answer just a cold stare, unconvinced.

"And Sarah, Libby's mum, you were there when she fell into the lake?"

"Shit of course I was, you know I was. I tried to save her, I'm sorry it didn't work but I did everything I could to save her." His mouth had dried now.

"And you saw her fall?"

"The rocks were slippery, she was panicked and frightened."

"So, you saw her fall?"

"I heard the splash and Libby scream."

"Okay." The policeman pursed his lips, made a note in his book.

On and on it went, and the further they went into it, the more he realised he'd been duped. He'd been a greedy, self-interested fool. The things he had done, the things he had hidden caused them to frown at him and he began to doubt even his own reasons for his actions. He began to question just how culpable he had been. If he had stuck to the rules and the guidelines, would Mrs Carmody still be alive today? Would they both still be alive? It shook him to the core.

He was terrified for himself and he wondered constantly what was happening with Libby, whether she was suffering in innocence as he was, or was her situation even worse, was she hiding guilt?

Eventually they let him go. "Thanks for your help, Jed." He nodded as he signed the statement, it was all in there, the subterfuge, the stolen desk set, the conversation with Sarah in the garden, pages and pages of illogical decisions and blind eyes turned. As he read through it, he understood that although he had been unforgivably stupid, Libby was in deep trouble.

It was over, but as he walked out to the car where his mum sat calm and quiet there was the other thing, the thing that kept him awake at night and ambushed him in the day whenever he allowed his mind to wander for a moment – the vision of Libby standing above him, her fingers over her mother's pale wet lips, the shake of her head. "I don't think it's any good. You tried, Jed, we tried, but I don't think it's any good. No, come on now. Leave her, it's over."

He had re-run it over and over until he thought it would drive him as mad as the poor dead woman, could he have done more? Had she indeed been hovering on the brink and had he let her slip over? Was he guilty of letting her die?

The next few days were confused and frustrating, they didn't know what was going on. Jed's dad brought news from the golf club. He had heard via the grapevine that Libby had been released on bail, but she didn't come back to the house. They were asked by the police to send her clothes to a hostel and then he heard that she'd moved back to the flat over the garage.

Eventually, he was called to give his evidence, to explain his behaviour, to admit to the way she had used him and taken advantage of his vanity and pride. His mum and dad were there with him every step of the way but he saw in the odd unguarded glance, the sudden quiet when he stepped into a room, just how he had let them down and it tore at him just as much as Libby's betrayal. For a brief moment he had been the hero and it had turned to dust.

* * *

Samantha was already in the corner of the pub when Jed arrived, she raised her glass and wiggled it at him. He ordered another white wine for her and a pint for himself.

She stood as he reached the table and leaned over to kiss his cheek. "Hello, you're looking well, Jed. Better than when I last saw you anyway. He nodded at her. "You look great. London must agree with you."

"It does, it does. You should come up, it's mad and hectic but I love it."

"Oh well, maybe one day. I'm quite happy at the moment though."

"How is it, your new job?" she asked.

"Yeah, it's good actually, I should have gone into straight surveying from the start, I guess. I don't think I was really cut out for all that other stuff."

"No, well." She looked away, couldn't meet his eyes for a moment.

"Do you see anyone from B and H?"

"No, not really, only now and again by accident you know."

"Right. And that other business, is that all over now?" He nodded and took a big gulp of beer.

"She got away with it all didn't she."

"I guess so. I never did thank you, for being there, in court."

"Yeah you did, over and over. Anyway, it was the least I could do, we're mates after all."

"Well thanks again, it meant a lot to me." For a moment they were silent, each with their own thoughts.

He had given his evidence and seen the doubt in the eyes of the jury even though he wasn't on trial. The papers had scorned his testimony, he was after all an estate agent and as everyone knew, they were dodgy.

He had though looked her in the eyes as she walked from the court. They had believed her in the end, that she hadn't known about the old woman in the cellar, had believed Mrs Carmody to be safe, somewhere else.

They had decided that the loss of her mother was suffering enough, and for the lesser crime of trying to defraud her aunt's estate, they had suspended the sentence. She'd had a good solicitor, after all Irwin's knew there was the promise of great wealth and the old boys' network hummed with information in spite of what they might say.

"She got the place after all, didn't she?" Sam said.

Jed just nodded.

"It was always going to be hers. There was the will and no-one to contest it. It's been sold. They're knocking the house down, draining the lake."

"Well that's good."

"Yes, too late though." He shrugged. "Just too bloody late. Still going to do the Hotel and Spa but all new, it's an outside company, strangers. I was offered the surveying contract."

"Good grief really, are you taking it?" He grinned at her and raised his eyebrows.

"What do you think?"

"Yeah, right."

"Passed it up the line though. One of the senior partners has got it. I might be an idiot, Sam, but I'm not stupid."

The End

If you enjoyed this book, please let others know by leaving a quick review on Amazon. Also, if you spot anything untoward in the paperback, get in touch. We strive for the best quality and appreciate reader feedback.

editor@thebookfolks.com

www.thebookfolks.com

www.ingramcontent.com/pod-product-compliance
Lightning Source LLC
Chambersburg PA
CBHW060519220726
48290CB00015B/2141